SEARCHING

SEARCHING

A Novel

D.H. Caldwell

iUniverse, Inc.
New York Lincoln Shanghai

SEARCHING

Copyright © 2007 by D.H. Caldwell

iUniverse books may be ordered through booksellers or by contacting:

iUniverse
2021 Pine Lake Road, Suite 100
Lincoln, NE 68512
www.iuniverse.com
1-800-Authors (1-800-288-4677)

Because of the dynamic nature of the Internet, any Web addresses or links contained in this book may have changed since publication and may no longer be valid.

This is a work of fiction. All of the characters, names, incidents, organizations, and dialogue in this novel are either the products of the author's imagination or are used fictitiously.

ISBN: 978-0-595-47179-9 (pbk)
ISBN: 978-0-595-71219-9 (cloth)
ISBN: 978-0-595-91458-6 (ebk)

Printed in the United States of America

CHAPTER 1

───────▼───────

It happened in an instant. Larry Foster was driving on Little River Road near a blind curve, preparing to turn at his street, when a large white van came speeding through the curve at his car. The sound of the crunching metal was thunderous. Larry heard Christina's scream and then there was darkness and a deathly silence.

＊　　　＊　　　＊　　　＊

He was aware of a flickering light in the shadowy distance. Someone was calling his name. "Mister Foster … Mister Foster … open your eyes, Mister Foster."

A nurse was stooping over him with a small pencil-sized flashlight. He struggled to lift his eyelids and focus his eyes, but all he could do was blink.

"There you are," the friendly sounding nurse said. "How do you feel?" she asked in a soft voice.

Again he blinked his eyes, not knowing if he was among the living or in heaven where everything was white. "Where am I?" he managed to mutter

"Pardee Hospital. You were in a car wreck. How do you feel?" she asked again, gently touching the side of his head bandage to make sure it was secure.

"My head hurts," he mumbled, his voice low and weak. He tried to straighten his arms to sit up.

The nurse said in a firm voice, "No, no, you mustn't try to move, you've had a concussion. We want you to remain as still as possible."

"My leg hurts," Larry said as he tried to move his right hand down his leg.

"You have a cast on because your right ankle has a slight fracture." She once again turned the light to check the pupils of his light gray eyes.

"Where's Christine? Why isn't she here? Is she hurt?" His questions stumbled over themselves as he thought of his wife being hurt.

"The doctor will be in shortly to talk to you," the nurse said; her head bowed not wanting her patient to see her facial expression as she fumbled with his sheets.

"Please, Nurse, I want to know. Where's Christine? Is she hurt?" His eyes became wild as he pleaded with the nurse. She walked around his bed and tucked in the corners of the sheets.

"Mister Foster, you must remain still. Doctor Huntley is making his rounds and he'll explain everything," she said without raising her head to look at him.

Larry heard footsteps and raised his head to see a doctor coming into the room.

"Good, I see he's awake, how is he responding?" Doctor Huntley asked the nurse as he took the chart from the bottom of the bed and studied it.

"Where's Christine—my wife? Where's my wife?" Larry interrupted.

Doctor Huntley moved to the side of his bed and put his hand on Larry's shoulder. "You mustn't move your head," he said sternly, trying to calm his patient.

No one seemed to understand that Larry wanted to know about his wife—now. Agitated, he asked, "Doctor, I want to know, is Christine all right?"

"She had gone before the ambulance arrived on the scene," Doctor Huntley said, shaking his head.

Alarmed, Larry's eyes opened wide, searching the doctor's face. "What are you saying? Gone? Gone where? Are you saying that Christine is dead? Please, Doctor, no … Christine is not dead." His lips trembled as did his whole body, not wanting to face the reality of what he feared. His chest heaved as the awful truth began to sink in.

Doctor Huntley nodded and patted Larry's shoulder. What was happening was the thing he hated most about his job. The doctor nodded to the nurse and she picked up the hypodermic, moving quickly to administer the sedative. The medical team monitored their patient until the medication eased his heaving chest and convulsing shoulders. Again he slid into dark solitude.

*   *   *   *

His eyelids fluttered and Larry opened his eyes. The room was dark except for a soft glow of light outlining the doors and filtering through the curtain surrounding his bed. At his side a small red nurse's button interrupted the darkness as though it was an evil eye watching his every move. But he was restless, something was wrong—very wrong—and it was lurking in the recess of his mind. Christine? Something had happened to Christine. He lay in the darkness, his face wet with tears that would not stop.

The door opened just wide enough to allow the nurse to slip into the room. She held his wrist, monitoring his heartbeat. "Am I alive?" his voice was serious—everything seemed like an unbelievable nightmare.

Surprised, the nurse said, "Oh, I didn't know you were awake."

He said in a weak and trembling voice, "You can turn the light on. What time is it?"

"It's almost seven o'clock," she replied and continued her examination of his vital signs.

"In the morning?" Larry wondered.

"Yes. Since you're awake I'd like to remove your head bandage. The doctor will want to see your wound," the nurse said.

As she was removing the bandage he caught her arm, "My wife, Christine ... is she ... did I dream?" The words stumbled, but his piercing stare sought her eyes.

She glanced at him and then moved her attention back to his head bandage, "Yes, Mister Foster, it's like Doctor Huntley told you." She paused, wanting to do or say something to ease his sorrow. In a tender voice she said, "The Lord only takes the good ones, I'm sure that your wife was an angel."

"Yes," Larry muttered through his tears, "Christine was an angel."

As they were talking Doctor Huntley came in. "Good morning, how are you feeling?" he asked.

Perplexed, Larry looked at him. "I don't know," he said.

"You don't know how you feel?" Doctor Huntley asked as he examined Larry's head wound.

"All I can think about is Christine," Larry said, his voice barely audible.

Doctor Huntley took a step back and with a compassionate look said, "It'll take time, just hang in there."

The doctor turned to the nurse, "His head looks good, healing very nice. I don't think there'll be any lasting effects from the concussion. Clean the wound, redress it with a smaller bandage. We want him to look good when his visitor comes in." He grinned and looked at Larry.

The doctor's remark drew a quick response from his patient. "Who?" Larry asked, showing the first sign of interest in anything.

The nurse interrupted, "He hasn't had breakfast yet, Doctor."

"I'm not hungry," Larry said. He kept looking at Doctor Huntley, his mind on the visitor. "Who?" he again asked.

"Your pastor." He turned to the nurse, "I see no reason that Mister Foster can't have his pastor visit during breakfast," he said, lifting his eyebrows.

"Yes, sir," she answered.

Doctor Huntley went to the door, motioned to the visitor and held the door open.

"Thanks, Doctor," Reverend Evan Charles said and went to Larry's bedside, tears streaming from his cheeks.

Larry and his pastor sat looking at each other through tears while the nurse finished applying the new bandage to Larry's head.

"She's gone.... Christine is gone," Larry murmured.

"I know—I know," Evan said, taking Larry's hand in his.

"What am I going to do without Christine?" Larry said in small gasps.

"We'll just have to carry on, with the Lord's help." Then Evan tried to lighten the situation, "She's probably showing that sweet smile of hers, looking down at two bawling babies."

"Christine was never much for crying," Larry said as he tried to remember the few times his wife had cried.

"Then … I think she'll be pleased if we cut out our tears and remembered the good times the Lord gave you," Evan suggested as the nurse brought a breakfast tray to Larry's bedside.

The smell of the food made Larry's stomach feel uneasy as he looked at the tray and then back to Evan, "I'm not hungry."

"It's yours, Caroline has already fed me," Evan tried to smile, "and she sends you her love."

"Thanks," Larry said as he picked up a piece of toast and took a small bite. "You know Caroline and Christine were very much alike," he remembered. Larry took a quick gasp for air, his eyes began welling again and he put down the toast.

"Yes, indeed they were," Evan quickly agreed, "we're two lucky men." He looked at Larry and negatively shook his head as he touched his arm, "We promised ourselves not to do this," he said as he wiped his own eyes. "Eat your scrambled eggs before they get cold," Evan added as he put a pat of butter on top of the eggs and another on the grits.

Neither spoke while Larry tried to control his emotions and began eating.

The nurse came into the room and began tucking in the sheets at the bottom of the bed. "How's he doing?" she asked, looking at Evan.

"He's doing fine," Evan answered.

Larry took a quick sip of his coffee and said to the nurse, "Would you please bring Reverend Charles a cup of coffee? We've got lots of talking to do," his voice sounded firmer.

"Yes, sir," she said and looking at Evan remarked, "I don't think there's anything wrong with his mind. Doctor Huntley will be pleased to hear this."

The nurse returned with a carafe of coffee and placed it on the bedside table, arranging things so that the two men could sit close, have their coffee and talk. "Now, when you need anything just push this little red button," she pointed to the controls clipped to side of the bed rail.

"Thank you, Nurse," Larry said. Looking at Evan he asked, "Are we going to talk about Christine?" His eyes darkened and became sad.

"Yes, we must talk about her," Evan spoke with conviction, "the more the better. To put Christine in the back of our mind does not honor her. She'd want to be right here with us and I truly believe that her spirit is."

Larry took a deep breath trying to make his voice steady. "Evan, why did God take Christine … and … leave me?" His eyes never wavered as he searched his friend's face for the possible answer.

"It's not for us to know the mind of God, not at this stage of life." Evan scrutinized Larry's eyes, then looked away, trying to think of words that might help his friend's understanding. "We both know that God sets up rules of nature and gravity. God's world couldn't exist without them." He smiled at this and took a sip of coffee. "And our actions must honor these rules. I know that I'm not gonna sit on a railroad track when there's a train in sight. The rules of gravity and motion says that I've gotta get out of the way."

Larry looked at Evan puzzled, wondering where his words were going. Evan sensed it, "You see, you and Christine were in the blind curve at the wrong time. It wasn't God's will that the DWI would come speeding into the curve. I doubt that he ever saw you."

Larry's voice was high and excited, "Are you saying that a drunk killed Christine?"

"Yes, he was charged with driving while impaired. Apparently the driver was on cocaine and I'm sure he'll face trial," Evan answered his friend.

The nurse opened the door and nodded to Evan, signaling that visiting was over, "Thank you, Nurse, we'll have a short prayer and I'll leave." Turning to Larry he told him, "I've other visits to make here and then at Park Ridge in Fletcher." He touched Larry's shoulder and said a prayer.

"Will you be back tomorrow?" Larry asked.

"First thing. I want to talk with Doctor Huntley and the best time for that is early—before eight o'clock. We'll be needing to make plans for Christine's service," Evan explained.

"Evan," Larry said as his pastor opened the door.

"Yes?" Evan turned and faced him.

"Where is Christine?" Larry asked with trembling lips.

"The police department called me right after the accident. I called Shepherd's Memorial Cemetery in Arden[1] and they confirmed that you had burial plots there, so I asked Shepherd's to take Christine's body to their funeral home on Church Street. Is that all right?" Evan asked.

"Yes," Larry said in a low voice.

"We'll have to discuss the service as soon as possible, but I want to talk to Doctor Huntley before setting a definite time. You rest and get your strength back ... and eat," Evan said in a concerned voice.

After the reverend left the nurse came into Larry's room and gave him his medication. Seeing how upset her patients were she said with an unyielding voice, "You can't have any more visitors' today."

"My pastor is coming back tomorrow early. I can see him, can't I?" There was anxiety in Larry's voice.

"Doctor Huntley will answer your questions in the morning. Your concern now should be to get plenty of rest and eat," she answered.

"And be sweet to the nurse," Larry managed a wry grin.

"Now that's what I call improvement—a sense of humor." The nurse looked at her patient and lifted her eyebrows to show her approval.

*　　　*　　　*　　　*

"How is he, Doctor?" Reverend Charles asked as Doctor Huntley came from Larry's room.

Doctor Huntley removed his glasses and shook hands with the Reverend, "Let's check into the nurse's lounge and get a cup of coffee." He smiled, put his hand on Evan's shoulder, gently pushing him toward the right door. "Amazingly well," he said, handing Evan a coffee mug. "That was a nasty crack he took across the head."

"I know, I got a glimpse of the wound while the nurse was changing his dressing."

---

1. **a small community a few miles north of Hendersonville**

"The wound is healing fast and the main thing is that there doesn't seem to be any brain damage ..." Doctor Huntley paused to sit down at a small table, "Of course, he has had the terrible loss of his wife—that's where you come in," and he looked directly at the pastor.

"Doctor, you've no idea how helpless I feel. I've never lost a wife of thirty years. Sure, there are many instances where husbands lose wives or wives lose husbands and each one is different. But Larry and Christine were close friends to Caroline and I." He looked away, "I can only be there." His expression was filled with remorse.

Doctor Huntley noticed the welling in Evan's eyes and the trembling of his lips. "You're a good pastor and friend. He's lucky to have you," he sipped his coffee and held his mug as if warming his hand.

Evan raised his head and said, "I've got to plan a service for Christine. When will you release Larry?"

"To go home or just for the service?" Doctor Huntley asked.

"Oh, I expect he'll want to go home as soon as possible," Evan said as he reached for the carafe and refilled their cups.

Doctor Huntley hesitated for a few seconds before saying, "That's not the answer."

"I don't understand," Evan said.

"As far as the head wound is concerned, it's healing nicely and the leg fracture is not that bad. It'll take about six or seven weeks. The cast is only to protect the leg and to keep him off it."

"Then what's the problem?" Evan asked in a doubtful voice.

"Head wounds are always dangerous. Their effect on the mind is unpredictable, especially when smothered in grief. We have to keep a close eye for signs of any possible brain damage."

"Are you talking about keeping him in the hospital for weeks?" Evan asked.

"No, nothing like that," Doctor Huntley nodded negatively.

"Then what?" Evan asked.

Doctor Huntley took a sip of his coffee and wiped the corners of his mouth. "He could go home," he paused. "What day is this?"

"Wednesday morning," Evan told him.

"Good, the days get away from me. Let's see, we could let him go Friday morning, if ..."

Evan began planning in his mind, "Great, then I could arrange Christine's service Friday or Saturday afternoon."

"You skipped right over that big if I mentioned, my friend," Doctor Huntley exclaimed.

"I'm sorry," Evan said.

"If a nurse goes with him. The hospital has a home care program where nurses go into the home every day to be sure the vital signs are checked and the patient is recovering according to schedule."

"Then I don't see the problem," Evan said.

"He needs a stay-over housekeeper," Doctor Huntley explained.

"No problem, Doctor. I'll have the ladies from my church work up an arrangement to rotate workers on shifts so that there will be someone in the house at all times," Evan said with a positive and assuring voice.

"Then that's it. You get your ladies lined up and we'll shoot for Friday morning discharge with his going into the home care program. A nurse will accompany him home," Doctor Huntley said as he rose to leave.

"I'm worried about his feelings when he goes into his home and Christine is not there," Evan pondered with a firm voice.

"That's your domain, Pastor," Doctor Huntley said, shaking Evan's hand. "I'll get back to my other patients."

"Thanks, Doctor. I've got to go explain things to Larry."

∗   ∗   ∗   ∗

Larry was staring blankly at the wall when Evan opened the door. His face lightened when he saw his friend.

"Good morning." Evan's greeting was warm.

"Good morning," Larry tried to answer in the same spirit.

"I hope you had a good night." Evan took Larry's hand in a firm handshake, "You look much better."

"My head feels clearer, not so flushed," Larry explained.

"That's understandable. We need to make some plans—if you feel you're up to it," Evan said, his attitude cautious.

Larry seemed to hesitate before saying, "I guess. I know that I've got to get past this, but my mind keeps going back to Christine, I still hear her screaming," he said, his voice low and weak.

Evan gently lay his hand on Larry's arm. "It'll take time, but you'll move on, somehow. With God's help we'll get by," Evan voice was strong and reassuring, emphasizing the *we*, wanting Larry to understand that he was with him in his sorrow.

Larry's voice was shaky as if he were not certain of Evan's words. "I'm trying, Pastor, I am," he managed to say.

"I know you are. How about going home? Are you up to it?" Evan asked with caution, unsure of what Larry would feel about facing the empty home without Christine.

"Yes, I want to go home," Larry said, but his words lacked conviction.

"I know it will be hard, but God will help you. I talked with Doctor Huntley. He'll let you know if you can go Friday if a nurse will go with you," Evan explained, anxious to see Larry's reaction.

"When's Christine's funeral?"

Evan was amazed that Larry was that far in his thinking. "Friday, Saturday or Sunday afternoon," Evan answered at once. "Which do you prefer?"

"Evan, Christine didn't like funerals. She thought them barbaric with all the sad songs and preaching. She thought of a funeral as a celebration of our life and our promotion to Heaven."

"And rightly so," Evan agreed.

"Then as soon as possible … and short—with happy songs. That's Christine's decision," Larry face was as rigid as was his voice.

"Then Friday afternoon is all right?" Evan asked, feeling his way along.

"I prefer it," Larry answered.

"I'll take you home Friday morning around nine or ten. We'll let the nurse follow in her car. How's that?" Evan asked.

"I'll need some help dressing with this leg cast on," Larry said.

"One of our senior ladies will be at your home. In fact, we've planned to have a care-giver with you continuously until you are ready to run them off," Evan managed a small laugh.

"You know I have no car, I'll need a ride to the church," Larry reminded his friend.

"Already taken care of. I'd better run along, I've others to visit," Evan said.

As he opened the door Larry said, "Evan?"

Evan turned and said, "Yes?"

"I don't want to cry anymore."

"I understand, my friend, I understand." Evan attempted to smile, but his effort came up far shy of its goal.

Evan went directly to the hospital chapel where he fell to his knees with audible sounds of anguish. He was praying for two friends, one gone and the other languishing in grief.

CHAPTER 2

───────────▼───────────

Two weeks later fifty-year-old Larry Foster stood on crutches before his wife's full length mirror on the bedroom closet door. His face was ashen and drawn, his eyes listless, and his thinner body made him appear taller than he was. There were more flecks of gray in his dark brown hair. No one would think of him as a particularly handsome man, but he wasn't ugly.

He shuffled to the front door to look outside. A heavy rain during the night left a thin mist on his hilltop. Grabbing a few paper towels he carefully pushed the storm door open with his crutch and went outside to dry a lawn chair before sitting down.

Mystically the thin wisp of clouds lifted as the morning sun heated the valley. He could now see Mud creek as it snaked west and upward, blending into the light blue sky. Gazing at the mountains in the distance he could almost feel his spirit escape from his body and soar cloud-like through the valley, down and up and descending on a tall pine tree on Sentell's Knob. Yes—and his mind continued its imaging, maybe Christine's spirit would go with him. Together they would explore the clefts and chunks of the enchanting hillside.

The creaking of the door interrupted his day dreaming. He thought it was the nurse for he had heard a car on the gravel. "A hand affectionately touched his shoulder. Larry looked around and was surprised to see his pastor and good friend, "Evan, good morning."

"Larry, a good day to you—and how lucky you are to have this view and to be basking in the morning's early sunlight."

"I enjoyed the service yesterday. Did you know I was there?" Larry asked.

"Of course, people usually sit in their own particular place which I don't particularly approve, but if there are empty seats I know who is missing," Evan explained with a smile.

"I left at the side entrance," Larry said.

"I know, you wanted to by-pass your pastor. Not a good thing to do," Evan cautioned with a twinkle in his eyes.

Larry tried to grin, "I figured that you had seen enough of me to last for a month or two …"

"Never. You're dear to me, as was Christine. It's very important for me to share your life. Don't ever forget that." Evan meant it as he walked to the front of Larry's chair and looked directly at him.

"I know, Evan, I want you to. In fact, I need you, especially at this time," Larry said with sincerity in his voice. He wanted to say, "Since Christine left," but was afraid his voice would betray his troubled heart and he wouldn't be able to control his emotions.

Evan seemed to sense his friend's inward thoughts and as he was pulling up a chair, said, "You're coming along. I can tell that you're gonna get past this crisis."

"You're trying to encourage me … and you are." Larry's voice was candid with a hint of enthusiasm, "Evan, at first I thought of death as a punishment."

"You can't do that, we both know that God wouldn't do that to Christine or you." Evan searched Larry's face for evidence that he believed.

"I found that out. Then I began thinking of Christine as God's angel—worthy to be called home. Slowly I began to realize that we were in the wrong place at the wrong time, that a drunken driver speeding out of control and out of his mind—all occurring at the same time. It was a freak accident," Larry said.

"And God will make a victory of it. Christine is fine, completely free of any earthly trials. That's done," Evan lightly tapped Larry's arm for emphasis, "now a wondrous future lies ahead. Who knows what the Lord has planned for you?" Evan asked with conviction.

Larry wanted to share Evan's enthusiastic fervor, but he could not. His voice was dismal, "At my age I feel like my life is on its way to old age and most of my real life is behind me."

Evan grabbed Larry's arm firmly. "No, no, you mustn't think like that. Men in their eighties are even fathering babies. And, with modern science," he vowed, "neither of us really know what the future holds."

"But you don't really approve of that?" Larry asked.

"Of what?" Evan wasn't sure of what Larry was talking about.

"Of men in their eighties fathering babies?" Larry repeated.

"Well, I was talking in general terms, but it's true," Evan paused, "I don't know all the answers. Every case is different. The point is that my God knows the future and its wonders. For Larry Foster it may be awesome. I can't see you as a pessimist, afraid of every moment or day. My friend Larry is optimistic of every minute—each day," Evan declared as he leaned over and patted Larry's shoulder. A car was heard on the gravel, "Are you expecting someone?" Evan asked.

"It's probably the nurse. She'll let herself in through the basement," Larry presumed.

"Is she still coming? You look great and there's only a small patch on your head. Of course, you'll have that cast for a few more weeks," Evan observed.

"This is her last day," Larry explained.

"Then I've gotta run, good visiting with you. Let's have a short prayer," Evan said. After the prayer he remembered, "My secretary has a list of volunteers who are wanting to take you out to breakfast, lunch or dinner. Anywhere you need to go, just call," Evan said as the nurse came to the door.

"Just leaving, nurse," Evan said cheerily. "He's healthy as a horse." He chuckled as he again patted Larry's shoulders.

Nodding at the pastor holding the door open, she said, "Good morning, Mister Foster."

"Good morning, Nurse," Larry said, reaching for his crutches to go inside the house.

"You don't need to come in, I can check you outside on the patio." she offered.

"Yes, I gotta come in because I want to make some phone calls," Larry explained.

*   *   *   *

As the nurse checked his pulse Larry said, "This is your last visit, isn't it?"

"It is. Your head is fine, you don't need any more bandages. When I leave you will be officially discharged from the hospital." She stepped back and smiled at him.

"Thanks. I do appreciate all you've done for me," Larry said, warmth in his voice.

"I've enjoyed it, Mister Foster. As is your place," she said.

"You're welcome to visit any time," he declared.

"Perhaps my husband I could visit some Sunday afternoon," she smiled.

"I'd like that." Larry's eyes brightened at the idea for he feared the loneliness of Sunday afternoons without Christine.

No sooner had the nurse left than the phone rang. "Hello," Larry answered.

"Mister Foster?" the voice asked.

"Yes, this is Larry Foster."

"Larry, this is Gene Link, you lawyer of choice," the man proclaimed.

"Gene, I'm glad you called. I was planning on getting in touch with you."

"Great. I-I … Larry, I'm so sorry about Christine," his voice sounded sincere with a crack in its tone.

"Thanks, Gene, I'm coping," Larry tried to sound upbeat.

"And I know that your car was totaled. I've already taken the opportunity to talk with your insurance agent at Farm Bureau. I hope you approve," Gene ventured.

"Of course. I am thankful for anything you can do. I think that I've dozens of things that need to be done and any help you can give me will be appreciated," Larry vowed.

"Can you come down to my office?" Gene asked, not sure of Larry's physical or medical condition.

"You know I don't have a car and I'm wearing a cast on my right leg," Larry explained with an apologetic tone in his voice. "I suppose I could call someone from the church and have them drive me."

"No, no," Gene interrupted. "Look, buddy, I'd love a drive out to your place—that is, if you feel up to it."

"Sure, Gene, that would be fine. It's lonely out here. The birds give some relief, but a friendly face is more fun," Larry said, trying to sound spirited.

"When's too early?" Gene asked.

Larry was uncertain about Gene's planning. "Are we talking about tomorrow or today?"

"Tomorrow morning," Gene said promptly.

"Around ten o'clock and if you've no plans I'll take you to Kelsey's for lunch afterwards," Larry offered.

"I'd like that, buddy," Gene answered.

"You drive, I pay?" Larry waited to make all the conditions clear.

Exuberant, Gene said, "It's a deal. I'll look forward to a very special day."

*　　　*　　　*　　　*

Early afternoon Larry took a plastic grocery bag from the cabinet and slowly worked his way down the driveway to the mail box. After emptying the contents of the mail box into his bag he carefully wedged the bag into the crevice of his crutch. Going uphill was tougher than he thought, but step-by-step he made his way back to the house.

The correspondence from consolidated Air Conveying Systems reminded him of a job which he had been working on. Disgusted with his not thinking of the factory he studiously went over all of consolidated's letters. Many were inquiries and applications that needed follow-ups. There was also a commission check.

Fearful that he had waited too long he dialed consolidated. "Hello, Susan, this is Larry Foster in Hendersonville, North Carolina. Could I please talk to Lou Kearsey?" Larry hoped his voice sounded business-like.

"Hi, Mister Foster, long time no hear," Susan said.

"I know, Susan. Is Lou in?" Larry knew it had been several weeks.

"He's here, just a moment," Susan said.

Larry could hear her telling Mister Kearsey that his southern sales representative was on the line.

"Larry, how's the boy?" Lou's resonant voice exploded.

"I wish I felt as good as you sound," Larry tried to sound chipper.

"Aw, come on, it can't be all that bad," Lou urged.

"I'm afraid so, Lou. I'm gonna have to cut and run," Larry said.

"You mean quit? Aw, no, I can't believe it," Lou sounded negative at first, then he became serious, "you're not going with a competitor?"

"You know I wouldn't do that," Larry said, he'd never do anything to disappoint Lou or consolidated.

"What's wrong?" Lou asked, his voice lower.

"I've had an accident," Larry answered, trying to control the sudden onslaught of emotion.

"Bad?" Lou asked.

"Bad. I lost Christine," Larry said, trying to cover the phone to hide a gasp that he couldn't control.

"Oh, dear Lord, no ..." Lou's voice was full of pathos, there were moments of silence as neither party knew what to say. "Are you still there, pal?" Lou asked meekly.

"Yeah," Larry finally answered.

"Are you okay?" Lou asked.

"I'm all right, Lou. The nurse removed the last bandage from my head this morning. I had a concussion," Larry explained. "I'm also wearing a cast on my right leg and it'll be months before I'm able to travel and work the territory. That's why I'm canceling our contract. You'll need to have someone servicing the inquiries. Do you want me to send a formal letter of cancellation or will this phone call do?" Larry said trying to be honest and wishing the conversation could be ended

"No, pal, there's no way I'm gonna let that happen," Lou exclaimed.

Perplexed, Larry asked, "Why not?" He thought it was the best thing to do for the good of the company.

"Look, Larry, before we found you we tried a lot of characters—none followed up like you do. Forget that crap about our splitting. It ain't gonna happen," Lou was certain.

Larry knew Lou meant it. "Thanks, Lou, I won't say I'm not surprised," he stammered.

"Forget leaving, pal, you take all the time you need. Just get well. I'm sorry about Christine. Things are tough, but you can get through it. You're made of stern stuff." There were several moments of silence and then Lou's booming voice came back, "Aw, hell, I don't know what I'm saying. I should hang up and have a good bawling session."

"No, Lou, don't do that. I'm trying to get beyond the tears—and it's not easy." Larry's voice cracked at the thought of big burly Lou Kearsey crying.

"Larry, hang with me, there's more to say," Lou sounded sure. "First, we'll service all inquiries from this office. If the jokers want a rep I'll send one from this office or go myself—understand?" Lou demanded.

Larry yielded, "Sure, Lou, I understand."

Lou was firm as he pronounced, "Second, you'll be paid every commission that comes out of your territory whether you service the account or not—is that clear?"

Larry couldn't believe what he was hearing. "Yes, Lou. That's mighty nice of you," he said.

"It's good business, my friend. Damn good business. We don't want to lose you."

"I've got to go," Larry's voice was a whisper.

"Just hang in there, pal, we're rooting for you," Lou answered.

When Larry hung up there were wells of tears in his eyes. He walked to the door and stood gazing outside—not seeing—contemplating the kindness of friends.

*   *   *   *

Gene Link was a short stocky man with brown hair and eyes. He had a dimple in his left cheek which was almost hidden in his deep tan. His personality was congenial and engaging, always searching out a friend.

Gene grabbed his attaché case and bounded up the stone steps to Larry's front door.

"Come in," Larry invited, cracking the storm door with his crutch and standing back for Gene to enter.

Gene stepped into the entrance hall, looked at Larry and then embraced him. "Damn, I don't know what I'd do without Eva," his voice cracking with anguish.

"We're not going to talk about the accident," Larry said. "We've got important business to discuss."

"Right," Gene agreed, "you lead the way."

Larry gave him a choice, "We can go outside to the patio or stay right here in the kitchen."

"The kitchen, I smell coffee," Gene grinned.

"I made coffee just for this occasion," Larry said, pointing Gene to a chair.

"Look what I found at Ingles Deli," Gene said, opening his case with a flourish. Inside were two cherry Danish wrapped in white paper napkins.

Larry filled two mugs with coffee, set out several napkins and motioned for Gene to take his seat.

Gene unwrapped his Danish, took a bite and then sipped at his coffee before setting the mug down. He took a deep breath and said, "The first thing we want to do is to get all of your joint assets in your name only."

"Christine and I owned everything jointly," Larry told him, "even our bank account." Larry's eyes took on a bewildered look, "Somehow I always thought that Christine would be the survivor."

"No matter how hard a fellow tries, the future always surprises him," Gene answered and then continued, "we'll need your house deed and papers on all your valuables."

"I'll have someone from the church drive me to the bank and get those things from my safe deposit box," Larry said.

"Tomorrow?" Gene asked.

"Tomorrow," Larry promised.

"That's right, I had forgotten—you don't have a car. As I told you over the phone, I've talked to your insurance agent, you'll get a check soon for your car and then you can pick out new car when you're ready," Gene said.

"What about the guy that totaled us?" Larry queried.

"I'm coming to that. He's been arraigned and the District Attorney is throwing the book at him," Gene exclaimed.

Larry frowned and his voice hardened. "He'll be found guilty?"

"Absolutely, he's already confessed. I've talked to his lawyer, it's a gimme." Gene rubbed his palms together, smiling, "And his insurance is a one and three."

Larry looked puzzled, "What's a one and three?"

"One hundred thousand per person and three hundred thousand per accident—and we're an accident," Gene said with confidence.

"There's something else I should do," Larry remembered.

"Christine's insurance?" Gene asked.

"Yes, I just happened to think of it," Larry told him.

"Is the policy in your safety deposit?" Gene asked.

"Yes."

"Good. You'll have to give me the policy, then I'll go to Shepherd's, get a death certificate and file it for you." Gene kept pulling papers out of his case for Larry to sign, then he leaned back, enjoying his coffee. "One thing more," he asserted.

Larry's face was blank, "What? I thought we had covered everything."

"The guy that hit you was on a job. The van belonged to his company." Gene slammed his hand hard on the table, "The company is responsible for having a drunk on duty."

Larry looked surprised. "I didn't realize that," he said.

"You didn't know it," Gene answered.

"No, I didn't," Larry agreed.

Gene again pushed his chair back from the table and faced Larry with a serious look, "What I want you to do is to let me bring an expert lawyer in this field to sue the company that's responsible. After all, you have lost a wife and suffered personal injuries, don't you agree they should be made to pay?" Gene asked, never taking his eyes off Larry. "Sure I do. No matter what I do with the money," Larry said, pronouncing each word separately, At least they should be held accountable."

"Good, sign here, "Gene pushed an approval sheet for Larry to sign.

"How much is this going to cost me?" Larry asked, hesitant to sign any paper without a full understanding.

"Nothing, if we lose—thirty percent if we win," Gene said without a wince.

"Thirty percent apiece or thirty percent for both of you?" Larry asked, wanting to clarify the agreement.

"Thirty percent total, for al legal fees in the suit. In fact, if this goes the way I think it will, it'll be a piece of cake and you won't owe me for anything for my other work."

Larry signed the agreement and pushed it over the table to Gene.

"Get your key," Gene said.

"What key?" Larry asked.

"To your safety deposit box," Gene directed.

Larry looked perplexed, "I thought tomorrow?"

"Man, I'm so charged up that I want to start on this today," Gene's enthusiasm was obvious for their conversation or the coffee had charged up his body.

As they were riding toward Hendersonville Gene said, "I don't think this will come to trial."

"Why not?" Larry said, realizing that there was a lot to law that he didn't understand.

"You've got an open and shut case. No decent judge would let it come to trial. It's a waste of the court's time, not to mention the taxpayer's money. Nope, it'll never come to trial. They'll settle out of court."

He glanced at Larry. "My friend, you are gonna be a wealthy man." Before going to the bank they stopped at Kelsey's for lunch.

*   *   *   *

That night while Larry was waiting for sleep he remembered Gene's words, "a wealthy man." That sounded nice, but it wasn't his search. He wanted the life that Evan said God had planned for him, or was it the impossible that he wanted—life like it was? He wanted Christine, but that was gone. His future seemed murky. He reasoned that he was feeling sorry for himself and it wasn't the right thing to do. That would be a stumbling block to his future.

There had to be a future. There just had to be. He turned on his side and hid his face in the pillow. The house was a silent witness to his despair.

CHAPTER 3

▼

The sun rose like a ball of fire in the eastern sky. Its reflection awakened Larry and he turned on his left side, not ready to face the new day. He groped for the remote control on the side table and, without opening his eyes, pushed the ON button. *World News* was on and none of it good, so he turned off the television, thinking he would go back to sleep. That, too, was not going to happen. He was awake and might as well get up and go with the current in the river of his life. He reached for his crutches and hobbled to the bathroom where he quickly covered his cast with a large plastic bag and anchored it with waterproof tape.

"Br-r-r." he shuddered, his impatience put him in the shower before he adjusted the hot and cold water. He savored the feeling of the brisk shower as it pelleted his body. An invigorating brisk toweling assured Larry Foster that another day was real and dawning.

"Dad-gum it," he said under his breath while removing the plastic bag from around his leg. He had forgotten to shave before getting in the shower.

He looked at his face in the mirror, surely things weren't that bad, he thought. All at once he turned around, thinking that he heard Christine. Larry hung his head and grimaced. He was always hearing Christine calling him and expecting to see her around every corner. One night he followed her voice to her rose garden —fully knowing it was an aberration of his mind.

In the kitchen he took his vitamins and fixed a cup of instant black coffee to put into the microwave. From the freezer he took a pre-cooked pancake and microwaved it. Then he sat down at the table overlooking the mountain's skyline to begin his devotion.

Before going to the patio he sprayed himself with mosquito repellant and grinned as he remembered the Realtor that sold them the house saying there were no mosquitoes in the mountains. There was a crunching sound of car wheels on the gravel. He couldn't imagine who would be coming this early, then he recognized Evan Charles coming up the stone steps.

"Good morning," Evan's robust voice said.

"Good morning, Pastor." Larry tried to make his voice sound cheerier.

"How are you feeling?" Evan said as they shook hands.

"I feel all right, it's just that this cast is cumbersome. I want to get a car and start going places, even work sounds good at this point. Your volunteers are wonderful, but I hate having to depend on someone else for almost everything."

"They don't mind. In fact, they're having a ball helping out," Evan said with honesty.

"I know and I appreciate them," Larry said.

"How long before the cast comes off?" Evan asked.

"I'm not sure. I'll know this week. I'm going to ask the doctor to take it off early and put on a lighter one that I can put my weight on and drive with. What do you think?" Larry asked.

"I suppose that depends on your leg. Are you putting any weight on it?" Evan asked.

"Yeah, every morning and night—and then some," Larry's voice sounded eager.

"If you're doing that much, it must not hurt," Evan declared.

Pleased with himself, Larry said, "Not at all."

Evan looked at Larry thoughtfully. "Now it's time to talk about Larry, the inner man. How's he doing?"

At first Larry looked down, then he raised his eyes toward Evan, "I don't sit around hating the man who killed Christine and ruined my ..." In an instant he caught himself, "I should have said changed instead of ruined, shouldn't I?"

Evan blinked his eyes and said, "Yes."

"I don't hate the man, Evan, I really don't. To hate has never been a part of my disposition. Oh, I had some childhood fights, but not anything serious and never any lingering hard feelings towards anyone." Larry's words were true.

"You and Christine had a son, didn't you?" Evan asked.

The question and rapid switch of subject was a little surprising to Larry. He hesitated before replying, "Yes, early in our marriage we had little Larry, but his lungs weren't right. He only lived for a few hours," Larry explained.

"Well, you survived with the Lord's help," Evan said. Inwardly he was thinking that some people react with anger when losing a child

Larry turned his head, thinking of the baby, "I still think of him and what might have been. What a comfort it would be if he were with me now."

"And you and Christine considered adoption?" Evan asked.

"When you've had a baby they won't even take your application," Larry's voice was low in thought.

Evan kicked at an ant trying to climb his shoe, "You're young enough still to have a family."

"Not with a woman my age," Larry said promptly. Then he added, "Are you suggesting that I marry a young wife?"

"No, no, they often come with baggage, such as divorce or children, or both," Evan told him emphatically.

"Don't misunderstand, Pastor. I love children. I'd love to have a child, but not one which comes from the battlefields of divorce. That's full of legal pot holes," Larry said.

Evan nodded his head in agreement.

"The idea of marriage or romance, for me, is out of the question," Larry said.

"It's early, time changes hearts," Evan said with understanding.

"It may, but right now, just the thought of marriage makes me feel disloyal to Christine," Larry vowed.

"Have you ever thought of how Christine would want you to react? She may want you to marry and have a new wife?" Evan asked.

Larry looked at Evan intently. "But Christine is not making the decision, I am," he said with conviction.

Instantly, Evan knew that he had said the wrong thing. He quickly touched Larry's shoulder, "I know, you must live with your heart." As they talked time rushed by. After a good thirty minutes Evan, knowing he should leave to give Larry time to think, he said, "Let's have a prayer and then I've gotta run."

"And I haven't offered you a cup of coffee yet," Larry complained.

"Next time," Evan smiled as he took Larry's hand and prayed.

✳   ✳   ✳   ✳

"I think I can walk on it, Doctor," Larry said with pride for taking off the cast made his foot feel good, even though the pale skin was sloughing off and the leg appeared to be thinner.

The doctor rubbed his chin in thought, "It does seem to have done well. Can you put your weight on it?" the doctor asked.

"Sure. That is, I think I can. I haven't had the cast off before," Larry said, trying not to say too much.

"Here, let me help you. See if you can stand on it." The doctor took Larry's arm to assist him to stand.

Larry stood easily, experiencing only a slight tingling in his leg. A proud grin crossed his face, "See?" He started to raise his foot.

"No, no, don't do that. You might lose your balance and undo all those weeks we've accomplished. After the nurse cleanses your leg we'll put on a semi-hard cast to enable you to walk. You'll still need the cast until you're sure of it holding your weight.

Just be careful and use the crutches for support," the doctor advised.

"Thanks, Doctor," Larry said as he waited for the nurse to equip his recovering leg with the new walking cast. When she was done, he thanked her and walked proudly from the doctor's office.

Late that afternoon, close to six his phone rang. The excited voice of the caller said, "Hello, my wealthy friend."

"This must be Gene Link, for you're the only person I know that talks about that subject. Larry's voice eager and happy for he was still basking in the joy of his new walking cast.

"Larry, I've just come from a meeting with a very large check. They settled out of court." Gene's words cascaded over each other in a joyous torrent, "They wouldn't let us go. I knew they were desperate to get the case settled today."

"That's good," Larry managed to get a few words in the conversation.

"Good? It's great. Wait till you see the check," Gene exuded in a loud voice.

"I've got some good news, too. The doctor had his nurse put on a walking cast and I-I …" Larry's voice stumbled.

Gene broke in, saying, "Great, buddy, but let me tell you that several times my partner and I picked up our cases and every time they would stop us from walking outta the room by giving in. When it went past five o'clock they got desperate. Finally they accepted our figure. They caved in, buddy … they caved in—lock, stock and dollars.—big bucks. I'm talking …"

Finally Gene ran out of breath and Larry filled the pause by saying, "That's good, I'm proud of you."

"Look, Larry, I'm running late and the little woman has set up a dinner date. I'd better run, but I want to see you in my office first thing tomorrow. Oh, man, this is so great." Gene couldn't think of enough words to express his joy.

"I'll have to call the church after nine in the morning for a volunteer ride," Larry explained.

"Oh, I'm sorry, I forgot. I'll come get you, there's loads of papers to sign. And, don't forget your safety deposit box key. I'll pick you up around nine," Gene promised. Then, before Larry could say anything, Gene added, "Or do you want to go out for breakfast? I can come earlier ..."

"No, nine is okay. I want to get in some early morning walking with my new cast," Larry said, before hanging up the phone.

Larry was glad to get off the phone with Gene. It was pleasant to have something planned for the next day and even better to get all the legal work behind him, but right now he was anxious to see how mobile he could be. Going up and down his sloped driveway he carefully walked to the mail box. When he got back to the house his face was beaming. He had done it with a cane, but without crutches.

Again an overnight rain had left the hillsides bathed in misty hues of silver and gray. The sun, a rising giant spotlight had begun breaking through the morning fog with streaking shafts of yellow and shimmering gold. Larry stared in silent meditation at the early morning wonder, thinking that only God could create such beauty.

Larry was waiting when Gene drove up. Gingerly he picked up his attaché case and walked down the stone steps to the car.

"Good morning, my wealthy friend," Gene said as he leaned over and pushed open the car door on the passenger side.

"Good morning. You keep saying that and I'll start believing it," Larry answered.

"Believe it, my friend, believe it. Just wait until you see the checks," Gene said with a broad smile.

Larry hooked his seatbelt, saying, "I've got to buy me a car. I'm sure I can drive."

"We're gonna take care of that," Gene promised.

For over two hours they drank coffee and went over papers. First they studied all the accounts that had been changed from joint ownership over to Larry's name only. As Gene explained each transaction Larry slipped the papers into his attaché case. Next, Gene began pushing checks over the table to Larry. He began with the one from Larry's auto insurance, then there was the driver's liability check. When he came to the big company liability check he positioned it and slowly wedged it in front of Larry's eyes. Like the Cheshire cat he watched closely to see Larry's reaction.

Larry nonchalantly glanced at the check and turned his head to the side.

Gene was surprised and wondered what was wrong. "Didn't we ask for enough?" His eyes blinked, trying to figure out Larry's reaction to the large check.

"No, no, don't think that." His eyes welled with unshed tears, "It's all so final."

Gene was flabbergasted, "What … what are you talking about?"

Larry slowly picked up the check and held it between them. He had difficulty asking the words, "Is this Christine's final worth?"

Gene looked down, saying, "I'm sorry, Larry, I really am."

Larry took a deep breath and put the check into his case, "I shouldn't have said that, I'm raining on your sun. You're proud and I'm very pleased with you and your partner's work. You couldn't have done better and I apologize. Please understand that I'm swimming in unchartered waters."

"I know, buddy. No need to apologize." Gene's voice was tender with feeling.

The meeting was longer than either had anticipated. They went to Kelsey's for lunch and then to Larry's partner" who promised to call him after he'd gone over the figures.

After they Partner's office Gene drove to the Cadillac dealership. "I want to go over there," Larry pointed to the used car lot beside the dealership.

"You're gonna buy a used car? Man, you can afford to buy the dealership," Gene exclaimed.

"Gene, do you know how much they charge for those new Caddies? I'm not going to spend that kinda money."

A salesman walked up as soon as they drove on the lot, "Can I help you gentlemen?" his voice sounded eager.

As soon as Larry opened the car door he answered, "Yes, I'm looking for a new car at a used car price." As they followed the salesman Larry whispered to Gene, "I can't call on customers with a new Caddie."

Gene stopped and stared at him, "You're going back to work? You can retire and never spend all the money you got today," he exclaimed.

Larry looked directly at Gene, "Yes, I'm gonna work. I have to. There's no way I could ever disappoint Lou Kearsey at consolidated. He has faith in me and I need to repay Lou for his faith." Larry's face reflected his determination, "My friend, I really do need to work."

Gene stayed with Larry until all the papers were signed and Larry was seated behind the wheel of his new used car. "Thanks, Gene, for everything," Larry said as he closed the door and buckled his seat belt.

After leaving his personal papers in his safety deposit box and depositing the checks, he drove down Greenville Highway. He stopped at Fieldrest church, wrote a check and handed it to Evan Charles.

"Wow, what's this for?" Evan was surprised and puzzled.

"My tithe," Larry said, smiling at his friend. "I don't know how I'd have made it without you and your volunteers, nor will I forget."

"That's the way love works," Evan smiled. "It keeps bubbling out, always working—ever reaching out."

C H A P T E R   4

▼

Larry Foster looked out the window by his desk. His driveway was clear—thanks to his neighbor who had scraped the drive—but patches of snow and ice stubbornly clung to the ivy and small trees. It was late January and fall leaves had long fallen. Outside looked frosty white as bushes nestled under the tall trees. Only the white pines, hemlock and wild holly remained green. Tall hardwoods stood out against the azure sky while puffy white clouds moved slowly against the morning sun.

Larry used to look forward to February for it heralded March. He knew that there would be more cold weather, but he remembered when his dad set eggs under a turkey in the middle of February. This winter had been unusually cold and above average in snows and strong windstorms. February reminded him of the anniversary of Christine's leaving and his approaching fiftieth birthday. He was lonesome.

*　　*　　*　　*

The bright sunshine turned the countryside warm as Larry drove down the mountain on I-26 and stopped at the Inman, South Carolina turn-off and bought gas which was ten cents per gallon cheaper than in North Carolina. His next stop was for breakfast at the Waffle House on I-85 North near Gaffney, South Carolina.

His light puffy omelet and black coffee tasted good as he sat and listened to the friendly banter of the waitresses. The name tag of his waitress read *Pam* and she was popping-out pregnant. "Can't be long," Larry said, emboldened by the other waitresses' teasing.

Pam wore little makeup. She didn't need it with her rosy cheeks, sparkling blue eyes, and short-cropped light brown hair. "I'll try and not have the baby until you finish your coffee," she snapped back as she refilled his coffee cup.

"First?" Larry asked as he wiped lingering drips of coffee on his cup with his paper napkin.

Pam looked at him, a slight half-smile on her face, "First what? Are you complaining because I spilled one little drop of coffee?"

"Watch out, girls, she's getting testy," one of the waitresses said.

"Next thing we'll see is her eating the food here," another waitress added.

Larry was chagrined, thinking he caused the teasing. "I didn't mean to cause a ruckus," he said. "I meant was this your first child," he explained.

"Honey, that's the sweetest thing you could have said," Pam said with a smile. "This is the fourth and if it's another boy I'm gonna send it back and order me a girl."

"Don't do that, I'll take it," Larry said without thinking. "You have three boys already?" he exclaimed.

"The wildest trio you ever saw," Pam's eyes grew large, "and I wouldn't take a million dollars for them," she quickly added.

"Your husband is lucky. I bet he spoils them rotten." Larry said as he took a sip of coffee.

"The only thing my husband likes is x-rated and I'm not allowed to talk about things like that in here." Hurriedly Pam reached for the coffee carafe to pour another customer a refill.

"If he doesn't like children, why does he keep having them?" Larry asked innocently.

"Like I said, he likes what makes them happen—see ..." Pam stroked her bulging stomach.

Larry looked down at his coffee and mumbled, "There are ways to prevent pregnancy."

"And—no—he doesn't like using condoms, if that's what you're hinting," Pam exclaimed without trying to lower her voice.

The only thing Larry could do was smile bravely and gird up enough daring to respond, "Actually I was thinking pills."

"I forget to go to the drug store." She stood over his table, holding the carafe of coffee, "And I'm sure this one will be a girl," she said.

Larry smiled, "I hope you're right."

"If you'll hang around a minute I'll get my purse and show you my boys' picture," Pam said.

"Fill er up," Larry grinned, "I'd like to see a picture of your little rascals."

After a few minutes Pam went out the door at the end of the counter and when she came back she slapped down a set of small photographs in front of him. "Be brave," she warned.

Larry studied the pictures. They were all healthy, good-looking tow-haired boys. "How old are they?" he asked when Pam returned.

She bent over him, so close he could smell her perfume, "From the top: five, three, and eighteen months," Pam said. She was close enough for him to see small flecks of light yellow in her blue eyes.

"They're fine looking boys," he said warmly. "Who do they get the light hair after?"

"Both their mom and their dad. Ander's hair is lighter than mine, so I blame him," she grinned.

Larry shook his head. "I don't know about that. There was a boy and a girl in our family. Neither Mom or Dad had light hair, but both of us had blue eyes and tow-white hair," he said.

"Who had the blue eyes?" Pam said, looking at Larry's eyes.

"Dad. Mom's eyes were hazel-brown," Larry explained.

Pam looked surprised. "I would have guessed that your mother had blue eyes."

"Nope, Dad had light blue eyes," Larry said emphatically.

"I think it's time for us to cut out this chit-chat," Pam said.

"Why? Is the boss calling?" Larry asked.

"Nope—the baby," Pam said as she hurriedly took off her apron and rushed through the door at the end of the counter.

Larry finished his coffee and as he was paying the check asked the girl at the cash register, "Is Pam coming back?"

"Not until after she leaves the hospital, her water just broke," the waitress said as if nothing had happened.

He lifted his eyebrows and exclaimed, "She's gone to have the baby now?"

"You got it," the waitress answered and turned to another paying customer.

✳ ✳ ✳ ✳

After spending the night in Charlotte and making an early call at Celanese Engineering office he went on to Columbia, South Carolina. As the miles passed Larry remembered the photos Pam had showed him the day before of her boys.

She was having another baby just as easy as shelling peas from a pod. If only he and Christine had children, Larry mused—a boy, or a little girl—someone to wait for him after a long trip, someone to hug and call him daddy.

On his way home from Columbia Larry called at Lockwood-Green Engineering in Spartanburg and chatted with his old friend, Don Keeney. "How long has it been since you've called on us?" Don asked.

"It's been over two years because Christine has been gone for two years this month," Larry explained. Then he added, "Why do you ask? I'd have come running anytime you needed me."

"No, it's not that. We haven't had a project involving your machinery. You'd have heard from me if we had," Don promised and scratched his head, "You haven't changed, salesmen came in here that I haven't seen in four or five years and I'm amazed at how they look."

"What do you mean?" Larry looked at Don seriously.

"You know—pudgy, red-faced, and all out of shape, but you're as slim as ever. You look great," Don explained, grinning at his friend.

Larry said, "Thanks, but I get lonesome. I live alone, not wanting to, but afraid not to. That sounds moronic, doesn't it?" Larry sighed, "And sometimes I'm acting like a moron. Friends think I should marry again or find a live-in bed partner. I can't do that." Larry shook his head.

"Why not?" Don asked. "Boy, if I were in your shoes, I'd be burning the candle at both ends—every night."

"I doubt that. You'd be looking for what you lost, but you've got your children. A waitress showed me a picture of her three boys yesterday and I've been envying her ever since," Larry admitted.

"If it's children you want, I've got four boys. Take your pick," Don laughed. "But seriously, don't you date anyone?"

Larry shook his head. "Nope, I can't. After thirty years with Christine I'd feel like a cheat. I'd just feel unfaithful to her memory. You'd feel the same way if something happened to your wife," Larry said seriously.

Don placed his hand sympathetically on Larry's arm. "You're right. I don't know what I'd do without Lois."

"That's my problem. If we'd just had children, but it didn't happen," Larry said somberly.

"You're still young enough to find another wife and have children," Don said.

Larry turned his head, saying, "That's more of a problem."

"I don't understand," Don's brow furrowed.

"If I found a woman my age she'd be too old to have children and I don't think she would take too kindly to a husband always mooning over his lost wife," Larry said.

"Then find yourself a young wife," Don suggested with a gleam in his eye.

"A young wife—that would only make matters worse," Larry said.

"How so?" Don asked with an innocent look on his face.

"How do I know she can bear children? How can I fall in love while I'm still in love with Christine?" Larry answered hopelessly.

"Marry one with children," Don responded.

"That's another can of worms, fraught with deep problems," Larry said. "Ole buddy, you're playing the wrong game in the wrong field," he laughed, punching his friend's arm.

Don looked at Larry and shrugged his shoulders, "Sorry, just trying to help."

"Thanks. I realize that, but you can see some of the problems. With a mother of children I would be the interloper, the children wouldn't be mine. I'd be in continuous trouble with and between mother and child." Larry feigned a smile, "Just the thought makes me mindful of how good my life is now."

Don pushed his chair back and looked at Larry. "It seems that we are back to where we started. I'll just sign one of my boys over to you. Or, better still, I'll let you support them all. They could call you Foster Dad."

Larry looked at his smiling pal, "I bet you would. How's Lois?"

"Just great. Every so often she'll ask me about the man from the mountains who used to drop by occasionally and take us out to dinner. Say, I have an idea— let Lois find you a girlfriend." Don's eyes lit up as if he had discovered the answer to all the problems.

Larry glanced at him and impatiently said, "Don, don't ever ask a woman to find a girlfriend for a friend—unless you want to end the friendship!"

Don smiled as he nodded in agreement. "You're right, guess I was fantasizing."

Larry moved his chair back, "I've taken up more of your time than I should have. It's time to move on."

"No, sir, I've enjoyed seeing you. I can't say I've helped, but I sure enjoyed trying," Don said as he shook Larry's hand.

Larry waited while Don opened his office door, "One more question," he said.

"You haven't learned, have you?" Don joked.

"Oh, well, what's one more trip to the water cooler. Might as well go for broke," Larry walked over to Don and touched his shoulder, "What do you know about surrogate mothers. Are they legal in South Carolina?"

Don looked at him quizzically. "What the hell kinda question is that?"

Larry chuckled. "Well, seems like I read something about couples coming to South Carolina to get a baby because of its liberal laws on adoption," Larry explained.

"You're not joking," Don said incredulously.

"Just a thought," Larry answered, hoping to end the conversation.

"Yeah, I remember reading in the news about surrogate mothers. If I recall correctly, some women signed a contract to be a surrogate mother and then after the birth decided not to give up the baby—or wanted more money than the contract called for. If you're considering such a move I can give you the name of a lawyer friend of mine who would know all the details. Better still, I'll call him right now, it'll just take a minute," Don said eagerly as he rolled his telephone index to the S's and quickly dialed a number. "Hello, Susan, Don Keeney. Is Sam busy?"

"Just a moment, Mister Keeney, I'll check," she answered.

Don waited. "Hi, Don, what's up?" Sam Simmons asked.

"I've a friend here from the mountains in North Carolina. He's interested in surrogate motherhood. Know anything about South Carolina laws on the subject?" Don asked.

"Yes, I do. Can he come talk?" Sam answered.

"Today? Now?" Don asked, surprised at the positive answer.

"Nope—not today. My appointment book is full, but we'll give him an appointment."

Before Larry realized it he had an appointment for next Monday morning at ten o'clock.

✳   ✳   ✳   ✳

On the way up the mountain Larry's conscience began bothering him. He was a victim of his lonesomeness. An errant thought had crossed his mind and he had given way to it by talking with his old friend Don Keeney. Now he had an appointment with a lawyer to discuss something that he wasn't sure he wanted. There was no doubt that he was a victim of his own imagination and loud mouth.

Disgusted with himself Larry tried to focus on the steep grade of I-26 as cars raced to keep up their speed going up the mountain. He always noticed the sign signifying the Continental Divide right before he exited the interstate on the access road to Flat Rock. Once on Little River Road he adjusted his sun visor so he could see the mixed hues of the setting sun. His spirits lightened. *So why am I worried*, he said to himself. *I can call the lawyer's office and cancel the appointment.*

He unloaded his suitcase and bounded up the stairs. "Honey, I'm home," he called out, but there was no one to hear or answer.

CHAPTER 5

▼

Saturdays were busy for Larry. After his devotions he operated the washer and dryer. That meant tearing up the bed and doing other household chores. If the weather was good he spent the afternoon working in the yard and going downtown to the dry cleaners for his shirts and the grocery store to buy groceries.

He always looked forward to church at Fieldcrest but on Sunday afternoons the solitude slipped in. He and Christine usually avoided the after-church crowd at the restaurant until three or four o'clock. She would microwave a bag of popcorn which staved off the hunger and gave them some quiet time together.

Without Christine, Larry had to fight his feelings of depression. This Sunday a battle within his mind caused him to debate the next day's appointment with Attorney Samuel Simmons in Spartanburg. He had thought of trying to talk with Reverend Evan Charles after the morning service but Sundays were so busy for the pastor that Larry chose not to. Anyway he wasn't sure that he would pursue the matter so he microwaved a bag of popcorn and found a game of football on television. Before the game was over he was dozing and Sunday afternoon was spent.

Monday morning he lingered in bed. His appointment in Spartanburg was scheduled for ten a.m. He would have to wait until nine a.m. for the lawyer's office to be open to cancel an appointment—that didn't make sense to him. He sure wouldn't like anyone waiting that late to cancel an appointment with him. Hurriedly he shaved, showered and dressed. If he rushed he could find breakfast on the road. He thought of packing his bag for a week on the road making business calls but decided against it.

It was a beautiful morning and there seemed to be an aura of anticipation in the air. He thought of taking the old road 176 down the mountains to Saluda and Tryon, but he didn't have that much time so he crossed on over to Interstate 26. *Oh well, I can visit the towns next Sunday and have a more leisurely ride,* he promised himself.

✳   ✳   ✳   ✳

"Good morning," he said as he handed his business card to the receptionist. "I hope you feel as good as you are pretty," he smiled.

She looked at his card, "I knew you were a salesman." She said and cut her eyes upward toward him. "Mister Simmons warned me that you were coming."

"Forewarned is forearmed," he grinned. "Just leave your pistol in the drawer," Larry joked. Later he might remember his words and second guess them.

She pushed a button on the desk phone, "Mister Larry Foster to see you," she said business-like. "Mister Simmons is coming for you," she said to Larry. "Please have a seat."

Before Larry was seated Sam Simmons came from the hallway with a big smile and hearty handshake. "You're right on time. I like that and I planned your appointment just in time for my coffee break. "Let's go around the corner to my favorite hiding place so we can talk."

He grinned as he held the door open for Larry and nodded to his receptionist, "Susan, we won't be back soon."

"Yes, sir," Susan replied.

They were just seated at a booth in back when a waitress brought two cups and a carafe of hot coffee. "The usual?" she asked, looking at Mister Simmons.

"Yes, Betsy." He turned to Larry, "Would you like anything, Mister Foster? I'm having a Danish," Mister Simmons said.

Larry looked at the waitress. "A Danish will be fine, thank you, Betsy." He had learned that remembering a waitress' name would get you better service but he reckoned that no waitress wanted her name yelled out if the coffee was cold or the carafe empty.

Larry turned to Sam Simmons, "By the time we drink all this coffee we'll be on a first name basis. I'm Larry."

"Of course—and I'm Sam," he patted Larry's arm, "and we have mutual friends in Don and Lois Keeney. Don says you are interested in finding a surrogate mother." He looked at Larry intently, "Is your wife unable to have children?"

"No, my wife is dead. I lost her in a car accident," Larry explained.

"I'm sorry," Sam said, leaning over the table, "I didn't know."

"You had no way of knowing," Larry said quickly. "Christine and I wanted children. We both had tests, but nothing happened."

Sam took a large bite of his Danish and wiped his mouth, "Why didn't you adopt?"

"Couldn't. You see, we had a baby boy that died right after birth. The agencies won't take your application if you've had a child," Larry said.

"So now you want to try something new with a surrogate mother," Sam said as he licked the last bit of sweetness from his fingers.

Larry looked intently at Sam and softly said, "I still love my wife. I'd feel that I would be cheating if I married or had an affair," his eyes were misty as he sipped his coffee.

Sam cocked his head as he looked seriously at Larry, "You're a smart man, my friend—a very smart man."

"I don't feel very smart," Larry said. "In fact, this whole business makes me feel like a fool. I should buckle down to life and stop moping around. I'm not the first man to lose his wife."

Sam touched Larry's arm sympathetically, "You are facing life. You're following your dream and moving on it." Sam looked straight at Larry, "Every man chases his dream. I see by your card that you're a sales representative. You represent some company—yours?" Sam asked.

"Yes, Consolidate Air—onveying." Larry wiped his sticky fingers as he talked. "I have a contract guarantees me commissions on any orders that comes from my territory, whether I sell it or not."

Sam beamed at his companion and asked, "How old are you?"

"Fifty and over the hill," Larry said with a wry smile.

"No, sir. Look how slim you are. How do you stay in shape?" Sam asked.

"I use to run three miles in the morning—four or five times a week, but the accident and a broken leg stopped all that," Larry explained.

"My friend, there's not many over thirty that would look as young as you." Sam nodded as though giving credence to his words. "You could have rushed to get a young wife right after your wife died and gotten into a mess of trouble. You know that in North Carolina a wife automatically earns fifty percent of her husband's estate the moment a preacher pronounces them man and wife," Sam thumped the side of the table.

Larry took a deep breath and said, "Yes, I know."

"Listen to what actually happened, years ago, in our office. It seems that this man of worth dated a local girl and they were engaged ..." Sam took a sip of water, Athen he became involved with his betroth's younger sister, married her, jilting the older sister. The couple moved to Georgia and the older sister married an older man and lived here." Again Sam paused, "Well, sir, in later life the older sister's husband died. The younger sister and her husband had an estate near where you live. The younger sister died and to compensate for his earlier jilting he married the older sister. They didn't get along. She wouldn't live in the mountains and he wouldn't move to Spartanburg. When he died he disinherited his wife and left his estate to a nephew. She sued and the North Carolina courts said that he couldn't pass on what he didn't completely own. That half of his estate belonged to his wedded wife." Sam paused for emphasis, "So you must be very careful."

Sam looked at his watch. "Let's get back to the office. I want to explain what we can do for you." When Sam arose and fidgeted in his pocket for a tip Betsy was holding a napkin-wrapped something. "Danish for Susan," Sam explained as he picked up the napkin and his check.

Back at the attorney's office Sam said as he was looking at notes left on his desk while he was out, "Two more questions. How are you gonna take care of a baby without a wife?"

"I take care of the house, I'll take care of the baby. When I have to make business calls I'll have a woman come in. She could also do some housework," Larry said.

"How much traveling do you do?" Sam asked as he scribbled on a note pad.

"More than I have to just to keep busy. The house is a lonely place when you're by yourself with memories." Larry looked down at his hands, "It leads to feelings of depression," he said as he looked at Sam.

"The other question," Sam cleared his throat, "have you any cost figure on this surrogate mother project?" He watched Larry very closely.

Larry nodded his head, "Oh, I know it will cost enough."

"What's enough?" Sam lifted his chin slightly, "have you an overall figure?"

Larry took a deep breath and sighed as he thought of his answer, "I know there will be a down payment and hospital charges. If I go through with it I expect it will cost in the hundred thousand range."

"Maybe more," Sam said, "but that's a pretty good estimation. That figure doesn't seem to bother you?" Sam always became quiet whenever he was talking dollars.

"No, that's a small price for a child of my own," Larry said emphatically. "It would be the fulfillment of our dream." Larry's eyes were misty.

"Then you've decided to do it?" Sam said hopefully.

"I probably will. The more I talk about it the more exciting it sounds. Maybe I'll regret it, but I'll probably be sorry if I never try," Larry said.

"Good. Let me tell you what we can do for you." He pushed two typed pages across the desk to Larry. "One page is a contract, the other is a medical form for your doctor to fill out," Sam waited for Larry's reaction.

Scanning the documents, Larry shrugged his shoulders. "A surrogate mother contract." A slight smile crossed his face.

"Exactly," Sam said. "It consists of three parts. The first part is the effective beginning which means your signature will be accompanied with a check which will be approximately one-third of your cost," Sam stopped and pushed his chair back waiting for Larry to digest the initiative cost.

"Give me some idea of what this covers," Larry said.

"Everything is at your expense," Sam said. "All you do is select the surrogate." Larry looked puzzled, "How do I do that?"

Sam leaned back in his chair again as though to collect his thoughts. "When I said everything, I mean everything. We advertise in newspapers, probably in Charlotte, maybe in Richmond or Charleston, if necessary. As we get names of clients we feed them to you."

"And I make the selection?" Larry asked.

"Exactly," Sam said brightly. "Then we go into action. We have arrangements with a local hospital to make tests on your surrogate of choice, to be sure that you'll have a healthy mother for your child. That makes sense, doesn't it?" Sam hesitated, wanting the importance of the statement to sink into Larry's understanding.

"It's crucial," Larry answered.

"Then we'll promise the surrogate mother-to-be enough of a down payment to insure her signing the contract," Sam carefully chose his words, "But she won't get the down payment until insemination with your sperm is complete and we're sure that she's pregnant," Sam meticulously explained.

"All those expenses come from my down payment?" Larry asked candidly.

"Everything," Sam emphasized. "Your second cost is not paid until you have a brand new spanking baby in your arms!" Sam said proudly as he beamed at Larry. "But—and this is a big but—you must never give the surrogate money. You can promise, but you pay us—we'll pay her. Do you understand? In other words this is your contract with us representing our commitment to find you a baby that you father. We make every precaution to assure your fatherhood. What do you think?"

"Good." Larry nodded his head in affirmation. "I never realized all these details, but I can understand their necessity."

Sam leaned back in his chair. "The second payment is the final payment for your baby. You promise to pay the surrogate, but you give us the payment and we'll pay her according to our contract. She gives you the baby—we give her the money as per our signed contract with the surrogate," Sam said firmly.

"That means that I'll decide how much the final payment will be?"

"Yes, it's up to you to decide how much you want to pay and the surrogate how much she'll agree to. But you must handle it through our contract with you."

"What's your fee?" Larry asked, realizing that there had to be something for the law firm.

"That's your third and final cost," Sam smiled. "After you have your baby in your arms our job is over. You take no risks, financial that is; if you don't get your baby we get no pay. If you do—our commission is net thirty percent." Sam leaned back in his chair again, "You see, the more you give through us, the larger our commission." Sam grinned and rubbed his hands.

"Sounds fair to me," Larry smiled. "And should the surrogate decide to not give me the baby? What then?"

"No final payment to her—no thirty percent commission to us," Sam said. "Of course, you are still the baby's father—we have the proof and surrogate signed contract. You have cause and proof for action against the surrogate. That means another contract with us. We'll discuss that if and when it happens—hopefully it won't," Sam said soberly.

"I see," Larry nodded. "But the good thing is I can only lose the first payment—and look what the reward could be," he said with enthusiasm.

"Well, if you decide to sign the contract return it with your check and your health page," Sam said, handing the papers to Larry again.

Larry shook his head. "No, I'm gonna sign the contract now," he said as he took a blank check from his billfold.

"Are you sure?" Sam asked seriously. "That's a lot of money."

"Money is not much without a dream," Larry exclaimed as he handed the check to Sam.

Sam's eyes widened as he pushed a button on his phone, "Susan, we need a witness. We've got a new client."

✻   ✻   ✻   ✻

Downtown Spartanburg looked brighter than Larry could ever remember, the streets were cleaner, the air seemed fresher. A man with a hope, with purpose and direction was walking its pavement—a man chasing his dream.

As his car raced up the Saluda grade Larry admired the majestic skyward climb of the mountain's heavily forested steeps. He wanted to pull off at the top of the grade and shout to the racing traffic, "Look at me, I'm gonna get a baby—I'm gonna be a father."

The search had begun. He had spun the wheel of his life's future. Would it make its stop on a fifty-year-old man's dreams?

CHAPTER 6

———————————— ▼ ————————————

Larry's exuberant feeling lasted throughout the week and he reasoned that it would take weeks for lawyer Sam Simmons to get some response from the ads for a surrogate mother. But there were many inquiries for air conveying equipment that needed following up so now would be a good time to catch up on his sales calls.

At eight-thirty he was able to get a call through to George Jenkins, Plant Engineer at the Ethyl Corporation in Orangeburg, South Carolina. "Mister Jenkins, this is Larry Foster, consolidated Air Conveying. How are you, sir?" Larry said in his business-like manner.

"Good morning, Mister Foster. I've been expecting to hear from you," Mister Jenkins said.

"Good. I was hoping that I could see you around noon or shortly thereafter?" Larry asked.

"I'll be free then. We have a meeting of Section Leaders this morning, but I'm sure it will be over by lunch time." Mister Jenkins chuckled, "You know how it is, when the men get hungry the talking stops."

"I can understand that," Larry agreed. "How about you holding off your lunch until I get there and we can have lunch together? Choose your favorite restaurant and I'll treat. Okay?" Larry asked brightly.

"Sounds good to me. I'll be here. Just come on out to my plant office, the gate man will direct you," Mister Jenkins said.

*   *   *   *

In less than an hour Larry was driving down the Saluda grade on I-26. He stopped at the first South Carolina exit for gas and black coffee in a Styrofoam cup and drove on south. At eleven-fifteen he took the I-26 south bypass exit around Columbia and reached the Ethyl Corporation Plant in Orangeburg at twenty minutes past noon. Quickly he parked his car, grabbed his attaché case and went to the plant gate.

"Mister Jenkins office is in that corner. George called and is waiting for you," the gate guard explained as he pointed to the right end of a long building. As Larry walked through the gate the guard called the plant engineer's office to explain that Mister Foster was on his way.

*   *   *   *

"Good morning—oops—afternoon, that is. You're Mister Foster?"

"Good afternoon. Yes, call me Larry. I'm sorry I'm late," Larry said, handing Mister Jenkins a business card. "I'm pleased to find there's a smiling face with a pleasant voice," Larry said.

"You call me George. Let's go into my office here and we'll look over the blueprints before we visit the site, okay?" George explained as he held the door to his office open. While Larry was being seated George pushed his business card across the desk and Larry slipped it into his case.

George Jenkins was a handsome black man who looked to be in his late forties or early fifties. His dark curly hair was peppered with gray as was his mustache and he wore gold-rimmed glasses. George laid out several blueprints, explaining their positions in the overall project-to-be. "We want to pick up' in this building and convey over these structures to this discharge," George explained.

While the plant engineer was explaining the points on the blueprints Larry took notes. "You are going to send our testing department a sample of your material?" Larry asked.

"Sure, how much?" George answered.

Larry pushed a brochure across the desk with a name and address to George, "Send a fifty gallon drum to this man. Be sure it's well sealed. We want to duplicate plant conditions, especially the moisture content and bulk density of the granular product," Larry explained.

George opened a closet filled with equipment and gave Larry a hard-hat, put on his own and they went outside to where the air conveying equipment would be installed. When Larry finished his rough sketches on the project they went back to George's office.

"Hungry?" Larry asked.

"Yes," George answered. "Do you have all the information you need?" George asked.

"I'll call it into my company this weekend. You should get our formal proposal, with prices, in approximately two weeks. It will be back in a week because they get their proposals out at the end of the week." Larry smiled. "Let's get lunch," he added.

*   *   *   *

Larry drove them to the hotel parking lot in downtown Orangeburg. When they were approaching the hotel's front entrance Larry noticed a lot of young black men carrying signs. "What's up?" he asked George as they were being seated at the lobby restaurant overlooking the street.

"They're from the local college, probably protesting being treated like blacks," George said calmly as he began looking at the menu.

"I thought all that protesting stuff was in the past," Larry said.

George lowered the menu with a pleasant expression and said, "Oh, yas-suh mas-suh," George mimicked, "but in South Carolina some folks still think of blacks as slaves."

"Oh—that attitude is dying out," Larry said, laughing at George's mime.

"My friend," George leaned closer to Larry, "I don't think there will ever be a time when blacks are really treated like whites—not in South Carolina," George spoke low.

"I suppose you're right, but it's different in North Carolina—rather, in the mountains where I live," Larry said as he picked up his menu.

Again George leaned over toward Larry. "Do you really think that? If you do, I've got some questions for you."

"Shoot," Larry grinned.

George looked directly at Larry, wanting to be sure that he wasn't offending his host. "You've probably got black acquaintances, but are they really friends that you have over to dinner? Do you go on picnics with them or invite them over to play cards?"

Larry stammered, "Well ... I ... I've ..."

George knew what Larry was trying to say as he continued, "You told me that while you were driving over here you were enthused about searching for a surrogate mother. I was pleased and amused. Suppose your lawyer sends you a prospective surrogate that's a black woman," George paused, anxious to see Larry's reaction.

Larry didn't know how to answer. He looked down and fumbled with his napkin and then looked at George, "I ... I ... don't know—I've really not thought of that possibility."

George smiled, "Well, don't worry, your lawyer in Spartanburg will never give you a black woman's name for a surrogate. They'll handle that little problem and you'll never know it was there."

*   *   *   *

George Jenkins' question had opened up other questions, questions that Larry had never considered—such as a handicapped baby being born of his sperm. It would be his child, too. Would he be prepared for such an ordeal? So great a decision. Larry didn't have an answer for himself. Then he reminded himself that Sam Simmons had mentioned a healthy baby, so his doctors would surely monitor that possibility.

CHAPTER 7

───────────── ▼ ─────────────

He had finished his calls and early Friday morning Larry was on his way home. A few more miles down the highway Lake Hartwell opened up into its glimmering watery green majesty as he crossed into South Carolina. On the other side of the bridge was a rest area overlooking the lake. Larry parked away from the crowded restrooms and strolled to a picnic table nearest the placid and beautiful lake. Looking back at the restrooms it reminded him of a hill of ants busily dodging in and out of their cars to and from the rest rooms.

"Taking a sunshine break?" a woman's voice asked.

Larry was momentarily surprised for he thought he was alone. He looked up to see a young blonde-haired girl at the other end of the table. "Hi, I didn't know there was anyone else down here. It sure is quiet compared to up there," he pointed to the restroom area.

"Traveling alone?" she asked as she adjusted a hair clasp behind her neck that kept her long hair in place.

Larry thought that her hair was probably bleached for her eyes were dark as raisins, "Yes, I'm a traveling salesman, minus the jokes."

"And always looking for some action," the girl said, watching his reaction.

Larry straightened his back and took a deep breath. He knew immediately what was up for he had been down this road before and was no longer shocked. He looked at her with a sly grin and asked, "How much?"

She looked at him and said, "For distinguished men—only fifty bucks."

"Fifty bucks?" Larry's voice exploded. "You're not at the Sheraton, you know." Inwardly the whole situation was ridiculous, but he thought he'd have a little fun with it.

"Well, a girl has to make money. We can dicker," she said calmly, never taking her eyes off him.

He knew she was local when she said dicker and probably lived nearby, setting up shop in the rest area. He watched her closely and asked, "Just where is all this action taking place?"

"We could go somewhere in your car and find a place," she suggested.

"Yeah, a one-way road in the woods where another car pulls up behind me blocking me in and I get mugged." Larry shook his head no.

"Then there's the van," she said.

"What van?" he asked.

"Over there," she nodded in the direction of a green van parked near the lake and beyond the picnic tables.

"That's yours?" he asked.

"Uh-huh. There's a bed in the back," she said. "I'll cut the price in half. Twenty-five dollars, okay?"

Larry shook his head and smiled. "Boy, you're something, fifty to twenty-five ..." he snapped his fingers, "just like that. Sorry, but you've got yourself the wrong pigeon." Disgusted, he got up and walked toward his car.

His lunch time coffee was getting to him so he went into the restroom. When he had washed his hands and patiently waited for the air dryer to dry them he walked from the building.

A man came up to him. "Say, buddy, how about helping out a veteran? I'm from New Jersey and my car broke down. If you could spare a little money to help get it fixed I'd sure appreciate it."

Larry suspected either a panhandler or wino, but he didn't smell anything. The man could be telling the truth—what's a dollar or two? As he started to take out his wallet the man's eyes looked beyond Larry and he suddenly turned away.

"Okay, you ... come on back here," a gruff voice behind him boomed.

Larry turned to see a policeman. Slowly the man from New Jersey turned and reluctantly looked at the police man.

"This man bothering you?" the policeman asked Larry.

Larry thought of drugs, that the policeman was suspicious because he took out his wallet. "I was gonna give him a couple bucks to repair his car so that he could get back home in New Jersey," he replied to the policeman.

"New Jersey, my ass. I want to show you something. Let's go over to a table," the policeman said as he took the man's arm and roughly pushed him to a vacant picnic table.

Larry watched as the officer made the man take everything out of his pockets and lay the contents on the table. "Your back pockets, too," the officer ordered.

Larry watched as the money pile grew. "How much do you reckon is there?" he asked the officer.

"Over a thousand—easily," the officer said.

"So, it'll take that much to fix my car," the man explained in an agitated tone.

The officer straightened his stance and glared at the man. "Shut up, you lying panhandler," he shouted. "I hate lying panhandlers who are too lazy to earn a decent living. You're scum …" He turned to Larry, "This filth probably makes over a thousand a day taking from honest people." The officer then gritted his teeth and turned back to the panhandler, "And don't give me any crap about fixing your car. I've been watching you. I saw you back up that green van." He pointed toward the van the girl was in. "Ain't nothing wrong with that vehicle. It was working fine when you got out of it." the officer added.

Larry put two and two together and tried to get the officer's attention, "Uh … officer," he said, but the officer was still railing at the panhandler. Larry waited until the officer ran out of breath. "Sir, I … I …" he stuttered.

"Yeah?" The officer turned to him and growled, "I hope you've learned a lesson, too."

"Yes, sir, I have, but …" Larry said.

"When you give them money—you encourage the lying filth. You understand?"

"Yes sir, officer, I know. But there's something I want to tell you," Larry said patiently.

"Then what?" the officer took off his cap and wiped his brow.

"Are you talking about the green van parked down near the lake?" Larry pointed toward the van the girl was in.

"Yeah, that's this guy's car." He put his cap back on his head and adjusted it.

"Well, officer, he's doing more than panhandling," Larry stated.

"Such as?" the officer asked.

"He's got a young girl in that van hustling," Larry answered.

"You talking about a prostitute?" The officer turned to glare at the man.

"Yes, sir, officer. She starts out asking fifty dollars, but her price comes down," Larry explained.

"Well, I'll be damned. Are you sure?"

"Yes, sir. I guess I looked like fifty bucks to her," Larry joked.

While the officer was taking the man to the green van Larry promptly went to his car. He pulled out of the rest area and stopped to watch in his rear view mirror as the officer walked to the police car between the prostitute and the panhandler.

CHAPTER 8

▼

Larry didn't have a headache, but many dark clouds seemed to be hovering over him. The passing days had caused him to rethink his search for a surrogate mother. In fact, he had decided to call Samuel Simmons Associates Monday morning and chuck the whole idea.

Saturday afternoon late he went to the grocery store. He was pushing his cart down the refrigerated aisle hoping to find some frozen entree that might appeal to his fussy palette. On the other side of the aisle a woman was bending over to get milk. She straightened up just as he got near her.

"Mary," Larry exclaimed.

"Mister Larry," she raised her arms and welcomed him in a fond embrace.

Mary was a black lady who Christine and Larry had known for over thirty years. At one time she had been their part-time maid. Mary's life had been one of hard work. After seeing her husband die and the girls leave the nest Mary raised four mentally impaired boys. Next she raised a grandson and for the last two years since Christine's death Mary began raising twin boys for a daughter who had children, but not a husband.

"Mary, you've done more than enough. Raising twins—that's just too much," he remembered telling her right after Christine died.

"Mister Larry, it's either me or the state. Their mother don't want them. She ain't gonna raise them."

Knowing Mary, it was useless to try and dissuade her.

Mary looked at him and asked, "How you doing without Missus Christine?" Her eyes were warm with sincerity.

"Not well," Larry answered honestly. "I'm lonely. Living without Christine is the hardest thing I've ever had to do."

Mary felt the pain of his heart and saw loneliness in his eyes. She let her hand linger on his, "You need a child, someone to liven your life. It's too bad that you and Missus Christine didn't have children. You are still young enough if you got yourself a new wife." She looked into his eyes and smiled.

"No, I'll never stop loving Christine. It wouldn't be fair to take on another wife while I'm still in love with Christine. I don't think I'll ever marry, not as long as I feel as I do now."

With a forced smile Mary looked at him, "Want one of my twins?"

"How are they doing?" Larry asked.

"Growing like weeds. Mister Larry, them children are the busiest I've ever seen. Talk about putting life into a place—my whole house shudders every time they get home. Them floors knows that they're gonna take a beating from the twin's running feet." Mary patted his arm, "I'd better get my groceries and get home while I've got one to go to."

"I'm glad I got to see you, Mary," he said as she began pushing her cart down the aisle.

"You just hang in there. Something's gonna happen, I can just feel it in my bones. The Lord has a plan," Mary said happily.

"Bye, Mary. Don't work too hard," he called out after her, "and get some rest."

Without looking back Mary yelled, "Rest ... what's that?"

Larry watched as Mary turned the aisle. *I'm lonely and she's tired*, he said to himself.

"Are you lost?" a friendly hand from behind grasped his shoulder.

Larry turned to see Hugh Mills, a member of Fieldcrest church. "Hugh, where did you come from?" Larry asked as he turned to shake hands with an old friend.

"I've been watching you while you talked with the lady," Hugh answered.

"That's Mary. She was our maid many years ago—a fine lady. We've kept in touch over the years. How are you getting along?"

Hugh looked at Larry, but his eyes didn't reflect his face's feigned happiness. "I usually tell people fine. You know better because you've lost your wife, too."

"Yes, I know. How long has it been since Edna died?" Larry asked softly.

"Going on six years," Hugh answered. "You aiming to find yourself a young wife?"

"No, Hugh, I don't think so, but I am lonely and it's getting worse," Larry said.

"Lonely? You don't know what loneliness is. Look at my wrinkles—getting deeper every day. I'm losing weight, ain't got enough meat on my ass to fill these jeans." Hugh grabbed the seat of his pants and wadded the cloth to show how much weight he had lost and his face reflected his bitterness, "Ain't no woman gonna have me and I ain't gonna have no woman."

As they were talking two children ran by screaming. A flustered mother hurried after them.

"Look at that. There was a time that I'd be enraged over such behavior," Hugh said. "Now I'd like to kidnap them and take them home with me. Anything to have noise in the house."

Larry listened as Hugh said things that could only be understood by another lonesome man. "Hugh, I'm fifty, and you?" Larry asked.

"Eighty," Hugh sighed.

Larry looked at his friend several seconds before asking, "If you were my age, would you take on the responsibility of raising a child?"

Hugh could tell that Larry was serious. He answered quickly, "In a fleeting mini-second."

"Are you sure?" Larry asked.

"Of course I'm sure, I'm positive. There's thirty years difference in our ages. If I had a thirty-year-old son or daughter now I'd be in heaven. You can believe the ass of these pants would be filled up." Hugh's voice was agitated. "Why is it that when our remaining years are few that we have to spend them in loneliness? A man would think, or hope, them to be sweet with love and memories, but they're not. Even though the memories were sweet one time, now that sweetness has turned to loneliness—sour and vinegary," Hugh said with disgust.

Larry suddenly felt like sharing his secret. "Hugh, I'm working on a way to get a child."

Puzzled, Hugh asked, "How—if not through a wife?"

"Surrogate motherhood. What do you think?" Larry asked, not sure he wanted to hear Hugh's opinion.

"Do it, if you can. You'll never be sorry," Hugh said with a positive nod.

*   *   *   *

Monday morning Larry was awakened early by the phone. "Hello," he said, trying hard to clear his throat from its huskiness.

"Mister Foster, this is Lucy—Mary Fox's daughter," the girl's high-pitched voiced wavered.

"Good morning, Lucy," Larry replied.

"Mister Foster ... Mama died." Her voice sounded softer and sad.

"Mary is dead? I can't believe it ... why, I just saw her at the grocery store Saturday afternoon," his voice reflected his shock.

"Yes, sir. Mama died yesterday noon," Lucy said, her voice barely audible.

"But Lucy, how? She seemed so happy and ... and healthy," Larry stammered.

"Yes, sir. Mama was always happy and busy," Lucy said, wanting to support her mother's image.

"Lucy, did Mary go to the hospital?" Larry asked, not fully understanding what could have happened.

"No, sir. You know that she plays the organ at our church?"

"Yes," Larry agreed.

"When the service was over Mama pulled the cover down over the organ keyboard and locked it, not wanting young'uns to mess up her stops. Well, Mister Foster—Mama started to get up from the bench and fell over the organ. I was coming down the aisle and thought Mama was funning. When I got to her Mama was gone to be with Jesus," Lucy explained with a sad voice.

Larry was puzzled about the cause of Mary's death, "But, surely ... something was wrong. Did she have a heart attack?"

"Mama worked herself to death, Mister Foster and she had high blood pressure," Lucy explained.

Larry could hear loud voices in the background. It sounded like someone had come into Mary's home and there was yelling and moaning, "Lucy, I hear you've got company. Thank you for calling me. You were Mary's favorite daughter and she spoke of you all the time." He said goodbye and quickly hung up the phone.

Early Saturday morning Larry made two chocolate-marshmallow cakes and took them to Mary's home which was right beyond the cemetery. He looked to his right, at the graveyard down the slight incline where two men were digging a grave. Larry parked at the corner, trying not to obstruct any traffic and walked to Mary's house. He had never seen the home with so many people in it.

The funeral will start in about twenty minutes," Lucy told him.

Larry hastened to his car and went to the funeral home. Every seat was taken except three in the back. Mary's body was in front with the casket open as slowly people viewed the body. Additional chairs were brought in as the mourners doubled in numbers. The preacher was white as was over half of the congregation.

I wish George Jenkins could see this, Larry thought as he remembered the plant engineer at Ethyl Corporation in Orangeburg, South Carolina who was skeptical about race relations ever improving.

*   *   *   *

At the Sunday worship service at Fieldcrest church Reverend Evan Charles' sermon was on abortion. At the end of his sermon he challenged the congregation to mentally make a decision as to the abortion of fetuses in four different situations. Then one-by-one he told of the tragic circumstance in each possible birth, going back to identify each birth. They were all people who had shaped world history in great and miraculous ways. The last was Jesus Christ.

*   *   *   *

Larry sat at his desk, taking pleasure in the beautiful skyline and the soft blue of the heavens. Then his thoughts shifted to his search. The past two weeks had again turned his depressive thoughts positive.

Mary had left this world as she wanted—happy and busy—with children. And there was Hugh Mills. He had provided Larry a look at himself thirty years down life's road. Surely anything—right or wrong—would be better than doing nothing and allowing life to slip into an abject of clinical depression. *If I'm lonely, then it's my fault for not correcting it,* he thought.

Then he considered Reverend Charles' sermon on abortion. There was no doubt in his mind that the spark of life is God's invention. Only He knows its journey, its consequences and its splendor. Perhaps his search was of God—that he was God's implement to something too wondrous for his imagination.

The search was on.

CHAPTER 9

▼

Several months had passed and Larry had forgotten to follow up on a proposal in Charlotte. At the Gaffney, South Carolina exit he stopped at the Waffle House and breakfast.

As he was walking from his car he wondered if Pam, the waitress, was back at work. "Pretty pregnant Pam," he grinned. When he left the last time she was on her way to the hospital.

"Good morning," all the waitresses yelled when he walked in.

"Good morning," Larry yelled back.

Pam was at her station and slender as a stick. "What are you having?" she asked.

"A plain omelette with as little grease as possible, burnt wheat toast dry. No butter and ... black coffee," he ordered.

"Grits or hash-browns?" Pam asked.

"Neither," Larry answered.

She looked at him, "Now I remember you. That's a weird order, you know," she said, giving him a sideward glance.

"You should, I was the last person you served before going to the hospital," Larry grinned for he remembered her well.

"Yeah, you caused my water to burst," she turned curtly and walked to the grill to turn in his order. She was intrigued at his remembering that hectic day.

Larry waited until she got back and began pouring his coffee. "I did not," he said with a serious expression on his face.

"Did not what?" Pam asked as she was writing on her checkbook.

"Cause your water to burst."

"I was just teasing," she smiled.

"I know. I'm joking, too. Well?" he asked concerned. "You did have a baby—was it all right?"

"I don't want to talk about it." She said, turning away and reaching for the carafe pot to heat up his coffee

He grinned smugly at her, "Another boy, huh?" he asked.

"I said I didn't want to talk about it," and Pam looked around to see if other customers needed a coffee warm-up. It was that time of the morning between breakfast and lunch when there were few customers in the place.

"You know whose fault it is, don't you?" he asked.

"You just come in here to aggravate me?" she looked threatening with the coffee pot in her hand. "Did you have to practice?"

"Practically all the way down the mountain," Larry said, smiling.

"Well, you're getting pretty good at it. Now, tell me whose fault is it that I had another boy?" Pam blustered as she cleaned off the place next to him.

"Your husband's—he's the one that determines the sex of a child," Larry informed her, raising his eyebrows.

Her chin was set, "Well, he ain't gonna do it no more."

"That's a double negative ..." Larry said.

"That's him—a double negative," Pam agreed, then leaned over to Larry, "but that double negative is gone ... out ... kaput."

"Has something happened?" Larry asked seriously.

Pam nodded her head, "He got a restraining order from the court house."

"Uh-oh, trouble in Paradise. Who's caring for your children?" he asked, trying to show concern.

"All he did was drink beer. He'd get drunk and start beating on me. I could take that, but when he hit my oldest boy I drew the line," Pam said, her face showed her strong determination.

"He moved out?" Larry asked.

"I moved him out—with police help."

"But your boys need a father," Larry wasn't joking.

"Not a drunk, they don't. Are you applying for the job?"

Serious, Larry asked, "Are you asking for yourself or for your boys?"

Pam, as most waitresses, knew all the come-backs, answering with confidence. "I could do worse. You're a bit old for a young girl like me, but not too old to learn."

Larry grinned, "True," he said, not wanting to get in a back-down game. He knew that waitresses always had an answer and one that might be embarrassing. It was time to turn the subject, "Who takes care of your children when you work, your mother?" he asked.

"Mom's gone. Died of cancer," Pam replied.

"Then who—a day care?" he queried.

"Nope, my sister who lives right next door prefers working nights, so she cares for mine and hers during the day and I care for them all at night," Pam explained.

Larry sipped his coffee and waited until Pam wasn't busy before beckoning to her.

"More coffee?" she asked.

"No, I've had enough. I'd like to tell you something in confidence," he spoke lowly.

"Shoot, I'll clean it up before I tell everybody," she chided.

"I'm serious," he said.

She looked at him, trying to see if he were being truthful. "Okay, I'll keep it down, but mind your manners," she threatened.

Larry was still unsure as to whether or not he should tell her. He groped in his mind for a beginning and decided to come right out with it. "I have a South Carolina law firm looking for a surrogate mother."

"Like in having a baby for you?" she started to yell, but remembered her promise and whispered, "Are you crazy?"

He looked straight at her, "I'm lonesome," he said, his expression unchanging.

Pam looked at him, "Yes, I can see that you are." Then she added, "But you're a man on the road. You can't take care of someone else's baby."

"It would be mine, too," he objected and then quickly added, "artificial insemination."

Pam asked in a sober tone, "But still, how are you going to do your job and take care of a baby?"

"I'd get a day nurse while the child is small. Later, I'd only need someone when I'm out of town," he explained.

"Do you have that much money?" Pam queried.

"I'm comfortable and over fifty. There are men who retire at my age," Larry explained.

"Are you going to retire?" she asked.

"I don't know what the future holds. I'm my own boss. As long as I can turn out the sales I'm a wanted commodity. I pay my own expenses so it's my business as to how I handle things."

Pam wiped the counter with a damp cloth and shrugged her shoulders, "Well, I hope you know what you're doing."

"When it comes to babies, no one knows what they're doing. In fact, most people do not plan babies—and if they do, they don't know what they'll get. You pay your fare and take your ride ..." he paused. "And put your trust in the Almighty, hoping for the best," he said somberly.

Pam looked at him, but said nothing.

"You sure you don't want the job?" he grinned, hoping to liven the talk which had become somewhat solemn.

Pam stepped back. "No way, when I got rid of ole beer belly I got rid of my pregnancy potential."

"Pays big money," he said.

"There's not that much money," her voice sounded adamant.

He took out his wallet and walked to the cash register. "What's your name?" Pam asked.

"Larry—Larry Foster," he answered.

"Larry, are you coming or going?" she asked.

"Going to Charlotte. I've got a call to make—why?" Larry asked.

"Coming back this way?" Pam wondered.

"As far as I know," he said.

"Stop by, I just might know someone who's interested in what you're looking for."

"Wonderful," he said with exuberance. "How late do you work?" he thought to ask.

"Till three in the afternoon. I come in early, before sunrise," Pam explained.

"No problem, I'll be here early."

Larry smiled as he walked to his care. There was a happy spring to his step.

*   *   *   *

Larry made his call that afternoon and spent the night in a Charlotte motel, returning to the Waffle House mid-morning the next day. "I have a friend who might be interested in being a surrogate, but I couldn't get a hold of her. Give me your phone number and I'll call if I get anything promising," Pam said.

A week went by without any word from Pam. In Monday's mail was a letter from consolidated Air with a lead from a chemical plant on Old Pineville Road, off South Boulevard in Charlotte.

Tuesday he left, planning to go by the Waffle House Restaurant in Gaffney to get breakfast and see Pam. "Good morning," the waitresses greeted him in unison.

"Good morning," Larry replied as he walked to the end of the bar where Pam was smiling.

"I just left a message on your answering machine," she said, pouring him a cup of black coffee.

"What's up?" Larry asked eagerly, knowing that she might have a search prospect.

"There's this girl Esther that lives near to me, she baby sits for me and my sister—a fine person," Pam said.

"She has to be old enough to be legally responsible," Larry interrupted, not wanting to waste his time on a teenager which he knew Sam Simmons wouldn't approve.

"Just back up ... and listen. I'll tell you all about her," Pam said. "But first let me put your order in. Are you having your usual plain omelette with burnt, dry wheat?"

"You got it," he exclaimed as he took a sip of coffee and waited.

When Pam had her customers taken care of she came back, "As I was saying—before being interrupted." She looked serious and he put his hands up in silence. "Now," Pam said, "Esther Mullins is an old friend, not a teenager. She's near her thirties. She did work in Cherokee Mills but was laid off. I talked with her last night about your ... uh ... project and she's interested. If you want to talk to Esther I'll call her right now." Pam waited for him to answer.

"Sure—yes, I'd like to talk with her this morning. I've a call to make in Charlotte, but I can do that this afternoon" Larry said.

While he was having his breakfast Pam made the call. She came back and quickly scribbled directions on the back of a customer's blank check. "Go into town on Highway 11 until you come to old number 29 Highway North—turn right on Cherokee Drive. You'll see the mill houses on your left. Esther lives in number fifty-four. All the houses are numbered plainly. You can't miss Esther's house, she's waiting for you. And, oh yes, she walks with a limp," Pam said.

Larry finished his omelette, paid his bill, thanked Pam and hurried to his car. He knew the area in that he had, in years past, called on Cherokee Mills. In ten minutes he pulled in front of number fifty-four which was in the last row of houses.

Softly he knocked on the screen door. The bright morning sun was behind him, making it hard to see past the door's screen. He heard footsteps coming to the door.

"Mister Foster?" a pleasant voice said.

"Yes, Larry. Are you Esther Mullins?" he asked, curious to see what she looked like.

"Yes, come in, Mister Foster," Esther said, unlatching and opening the screen door. "Please have a seat," she added.

It was a neat front room with an overstuffed sofa and two chairs. A small fireplace with a white painted mantle on the back side of the room had an ancient picture of President Franklin D. Roosevelt. Larry had seen dozens of these same pictures on mill houses where he grew up. He smiled as he was standing on a hand braided rug, lying in the center of the room. "This sure brings back memories," he said, smiling.

"It was Mom or Grandmama's rug. I'm not sure which," Esther said. "Can I get you something to drink? I have instant coffee ..." she said.

"That's all I drink at home. I rushed over here as soon as Pam made the call. Yes, I'd like a cup of coffee—black—no cream or sugar," Larry answered.

As Esther left the room Larry noticed her limp. It looked like a club foot, but she could have been in an accident. Esther was a plain, exceptionally clean-looking medium built woman who looked to be in her early thirties. Her light brown hair was neatly brushed back into a tight bun and her hazel eyes sparkled as did her personality. As they talked, her warmth of spirit pervaded their conversation.

Larry instantly liked Esther and had trouble bringing up the purpose of his visit. He wiped his mouth with the small white paper napkin she had given him with the coffee and cleared his throat. "Well, now ... I suppose that we should talk about the purpose of my visit," he said awkwardly.

"I've never thought of doing anything like this. Frankly, I don't know if I can, physically or mentally," Esther said straightforward.

"I understand," Larry said. "You've never been married?"

"Never married, never dated. You see, Mister Foster, I lived with my mother and cared for her till she died. I never knew my father. He left Mother before I was born," Esther explained.

"So you don't know if you can have children or not?" Larry asked.

"No, sir, and I want to be honest with you—I don't know how I'd react to having a child and then giving it up. Frankly the thought bothers me." Esther looked at him with uncertain openness.

Larry was touched by her expression of honest uncertainty. "Esther, I've never done this either, not ever considered it. All I know is that it will be done business-like. The insemination will be done in a doctor's office. I'm told that it will be like a physical. It shouldn't cause you embarrassment," he explained and then told her about his arrangement with Samuel Simmons Associates.

When he had finished Esther said, "And if we do this I will have a baby, which poses several problems," she said.

"Such as?" Larry asked.

"Would I be able to honor the contract and give up the baby? I've never been in such a state. Honestly, I feel I would honor my word, but it's hard to know what I'd actually do. I need the money—I have the time—but ... but ...?" Esther turned her head from side-to-side, mirroring the confusion in her mind.

"You mentioned several problems," Larry reminded her.

"Yes, if something happened to you I'd be left with a child I couldn't afford to raise. What if the baby was born with a defect?" She looked at Larry with a help-less expression on her face.

Larry looked down at his hands, trying to think of the right words to say, hoping to relieve Esther's perplexity. For a few seconds there was silence. Then he looked up and said, "I'm sure these questions will be answered by the lawyers and I assure you that they will be answered honestly. Even so, there could be mis-haps." He looked at her directly, saying, "Esther, I've never been down this path. I don't know how I'll act either. I do know that the answers are with a perfect God has perfect answers. I like to think that this is all due to His leading—that something miraculous will surely come of it. But, at this point, I don't know. I do know that I'm in the stream and the current keeps pushing me along. I may get out of the water at any point, but I just don't know when or how. I can promise you that I would never want to leave you with any financial burden," Larry con-cluded. "Precautions will be taken and assurances given," he said solemnly.

Larry slapped his knees, preparing to rise from the large over-stuffed chair. She was still smiling. They arose from their seats together. Larry looked steadily into her eyes and said, "Shall I give your name to Samuel Simmons Associates?"

Esther's eyes were glistening, "Yes. Isn't it exciting? I would always hate myself for not trying, so ... yes, yes!" Esther exclaimed.

"You may not be chosen," Larry warned.

"I know, but I'll have tried. If this doesn't happen, you've given me courage enough to go somewhere else with my life. Thank you again, Mister Foster." She shook his hand.

"Thank you, Esther," he smiled and left.

*   *   *   *

Larry made his calls on Old Pineville Road after which he spent the night at a motel on South Boulevard.

The next morning he had breakfast at the Waffle House with Pam and told her how much he enjoyed meeting Esther Mullins. "Tell me," he said, "is Esther's limp from a club foot?"

"I don't really know. She's so sweet that you forget about her limp," Pam said.

*   *   *   *

From Gaffney Larry went to Spartanburg for he wanted to talk to Sam Simmons about Esther Mullins.

"You mean you have a prospect before we receive a response from our ads?" Sam said enthusiastically.

"This came through a friend in whom I confided," Larry said.

"Then you've interviewed her?" Sam surmised.

"Yes. Esther is a fine woman who's been treated kinda rough by life's circumstances," Larry explained.

"That comes to many people in various degrees," Sam responded. "Often times that makes the person stronger in character."

"I believe that's what happened with Esther Mullins," Larry agreed.

"Then you would approve her as your surrogate mother?" Sam asked seriously.

"Yes, but with reservations," Larry answered, his voice hesitant.

"Oh ...?" Sam leaned forward in his chair.

"Look, Sam—Esther would make a fine mother—I'd be pleased to have her as the mother of my child," Larry said.

"So ... what's the hold back?" Sam asked.

"She's never had a child. She doesn't realize how hard it would be to have a child and then have to give it up. In fact, I don't think she would be able to, knowing she signed the contract."

"You're right, that's a real possibility," Sam agreed.

"Aside from that, I'd feel lower than dirt asking her to give up the baby," Larry said sadly.

Sam leaned back in his chair and grinned, "Why don't you marry her?"

Larry took a deep breath, "And maybe have a child by parents not in love?" Larry turned his head back and forth slowly. "And, there's the fact that we don't know for a fact that she can have children," Larry continued his explaining.

"No, we don't, but it does look as though your Esther is an excellent prospect. We'll bring her in and make a judgment," Sam suggested.

"If you do, send someone for her. I don't want her to suffer a financial burden because of this. I'll pay the bill for a private chauffeur," Larry said.

"Don't worry, well handle it," Sam promised.

As Larry was leaving he turned and said to Sam, "Is club-foot a heredity trait?"

Sam shook his head. "We'd best have the doctor answer that."

Thoughts of Esther Mullins bothered Larry as he drove home. He couldn't think of a thing against her. The club foot bothered him, but here was a woman alone who would surely be blessed to have a child. How could he take it from her? He couldn't. Then he recalled Sam's words, said in jest, "Why don't you marry her?"

Larry shook his head as if to give up on the whole situation, Esther Mullins and Sam Simmons. *Oh, well*, he said to himself, *Something else to muddle my subconscious.*

CHAPTER 10

▼

In Tuesday's mail was an envelope containing a slip of paper with a note from Samuel Simmons Associates. *Dear Larry, Our first response to ad enclosed. Doesn't look promising—see bottom of slip. Use your own judgment, Good Luck, Sam.*

When Larry hastily examined the slip of paper he only saw the name, address and phone number—then he saw what Sam meant. At the bottom, in a fine shaky hand, was written, "This is my husband's idea."

He called the number late that afternoon, knowing that he could drive to Charlotte easily in three hours. It was an unusual exchange for Charlotte. He examined the phone book and decided it was an exchange from a farm community north of Huntersville.

"Hello," a small weak voice answered.

"This is Larry Foster, the man who ran the ad in the *Charlotte Observer* newspaper. Are you Mrs. Josie Moon?" he said business-like.

"Yes, but you'll have to talk with my husband, Rufus," she said and put down the phone.

Larry could hear children arguing in the background. Then there was a loud banging of the telephone and a young voice said, "El-lo." Larry chuckled, he knew that a small child was playing with the phone. Abruptly a loud voice boomed, "This here is Rufus Moon. Are you the man to talk to about the new tractor?"

Larry was shocked at the question, "Well … no," he faltered.

"Then who the hell are you?" the voice demanded.

"Larry Foster." Larry blinked his eyes, trying to get his words right, "I put the ad in the paper for a surrogate mother." He pronounced the words slowly to be sure he was correctly understood.

Rufus chuckled, "That's what I just said. You musta been bending the elbow a little late last night, huh?"

Larry was cautious, "You mean drinking?"

"That's whut some folks calls it," Rufus said. "I calls it moonshining at midnight."

"Sorry to disappoint you, Mister Moon. I don't drink," Larry said.

"But you are the man that wants to barter with me?" Rufus said in a demanding tone of voice.

"I suppose you could call it bartering," Larry admitted, "but I'm looking for a surrogate mother to have my child."

"That's exactly what I said. We're planning to give you a baby fer a tractor."

"No, Mister Moon, that's not how it works." Larry tried to choose the right words, "I'm looking for a woman to be artificially inseminated with my sperm and bear me my baby."

"Hey, now … don't nobody ruckus-in' with my Josie but me." Rufus' voice was loud and certain.

"You don't understand, Mister Moon. A medical doctor will do the insemination in a medical facility. It will be like your wife having a medical examination," Larry explained tediously.

"What's a fal-licity?" Rufus asked.

"That's … ah … ah—like a doctor's office or hospital." Larry closed his eyes, wondering if he was hallucinating.

"Josie, hush them babies down. I can't here this man talk," Rufus' muffled voice could be heard over the phone. "Now then, Mister Foster, what kinda tractor are you aimin' to get me?" Rufus demanded.

Larry took a deep breath and answered, "Mister Moon, I'm not buying you a tractor. We will pay for all expenses, plus an amount to the mother for carrying the child." Larry prayed that Rufus would understand.

"How much?" Rufus answered quickly.

"All that will be determined later. At this point we're being a bit premature," Larry said.

"No, no … Josie don't have babies like that," Rufus objected.

"Like what?" Larry asked in that he couldn't imagine just what Rufus was talking about.

"Them prematures. No, sir, my Josie does things right. She lets them seeds stay till they're ready to just pop out—like peas in a pod. They's just pops out," Rufus repeated.

There was a compulsion to hang up the phone and forget about the Moons but Larry was curious to see what they looked like. He had started this thing and he had an obligation to Samuel Simmons Associates. They went into the contract with considerable time and effort on their part and he should act likewise.

"Mister Moon, you misunderstand. What I meant was that we should get together and talk to see if we can proceed with this matter."

"That's what Josie and me's gonna do. We ain't gonna do it less I gits a new tractor outta the deal. It might cost near to twenty thousand," Rufus said.

"That sounds reasonable," Larry agreed

"Then it could go as high as twenty-five," Rufus felt his way along in his bartering.

Larry could have kicked himself for allowing the conversation to continue as long as it had. It was hopeless as far as he was concerned so he politely said to Rufus, "I'm sorry, Mister Moon, but your wife would not meet our qualifications."

"Why not?" Rufus roared.

"It's just that we have a regulation against tractors," Larry hastily said and added, "goodnight," before hanging up the phone.

Larry drove north to Mooreville, made a business call and took I-77 South toward Charlotte. He was back in Gaffney, South Carolina a little past three o'clock.

Stopping at the Waffle House Restaurant he asked a waitress, "Where's Pam?"

"Took the afternoon off," one of the waitresses answered.

"Is she sick?" he looked concerned.

"You might say that," she said.

"What's wrong?" Larry persisted.

"She's sick of her husband," the waitress whispered and added with a smile, "but she got the medicine."

"What medicine?" Larry whispered back.

"A divorce," she raised her eyebrows.

"She's divorcing him?" he asked.

"Right," the waitress said as she went to a table to serve a couple who had just taken a seat.

*   *   *   *

Sounds of rain tinkling against the bow window and the storm drains kept interrupting Larry's consciousness throughout the night. As the sun disturbed the eastern skyline with piercing shafts of lustrous beams he turned on his side to escape their glare.

Later Larry arose from bed, put on his slippers and went to the front yard to view the valley below Sentell's Knob. His hilltop lawn was bathed in luminous sunlight, touching each lingering rain drop with resplendent brightness. Wisps of moving clouds moved upward from the valley to clear his view, and he was enraptured by flickering dew-dust that seemed turbulent in a frenzied attempt to make a form.

He looked skyward and there, on each side, was a beautiful woman with giant wings. The wings were of silvery form and ribbed with light golden membranes. They were dressed in radiant silver and gold. On Larry's left was a light haired ladyfly while the dark-haired one touched his right arm. Both smiled and grasped his hand.

As Larry often did while looking out over the valley, he thought how exhilarating it would be to lift out his arms, catch the angel and soar over the valley. The ladyflies sensed his longing and slowly lifted his arms. Before Larry knew what was happening he was in the air buffeted by a warm breeze, escaping skyward. His companions lifted their wings, floating gracefully in the airstream. Rapturous feelings swept through his body as he floated over Mud creek Canyon, past Sentell's Knob's toward the western dark side of the mountain and then back into the sunshine.

Before them lay the forestland with a solid curtain of dark green until they reached an opening in the forest curtain and there a secluded glade where deer grazed in the open meadowland. At one end of the glade was a rocky glistening waterfall with clear water gushing down the hillside and forming a stream which bottomed out into a small pool. Large rounded rocks lined the side of the stream.

Larry could see something, or someone, sitting on the first rock, but they were too far away to make out the object. Both ladyflies looked at him and nodded. Their flight flattened out and they flew earthward. Before Larry knew it his feet touched the verdant earth and he was standing in front of a tiny girl, sitting on the rounded rock. Her hair was light yellow and her large eyes were a soft shade of gray. Her delicate blue dress was white and with canary yellow lacing giving the small child an angelic aura.

So strong was her captivating charisma that Larry wanted to take the child in his arms, but something held him back. "Who are you, little angel?" he asked.

Larry felt like he was using mental telepathy His voice made no sound, but he heard her answer, "Aw, Daddy, you know who I am." She giggled and batted her light eyelashes at him.

Larry was perplexed, words like where and how flowed through his mind. "No, honey, no, I'm not your daddy," he explained cautiously so as not to alarm the girl.

"Daddy … my daddy … you are my daddy." In his mind he could hear her voice raise as if she was screaming, tears welling in her eyes and cascaded down her soft velvety cheeks. She appeared to have heard something and turned to look behind her.

A little boy, older than the little girl, popped his head up, singing, "Daddy, our dear daddy. You're the only daddy on earth for us."

There was something about the boy that looked familiar, but Larry's memory failed him. Before he could grasp the happening other heads began popping up from behind the rocks, singing the daddy song.

Bewildered, Larry could only stand and watch as an adult woman suddenly appeared and al the children gathered around her. She lifted the little girl and with tenderness dried her eyes with kisses.

"Daddy's funning us, Mommie," the child sniffed.

"There, there, if he was funning you he didn't mean to make you cry," she said as she touched the child's back in a soothing manner.

Larry strained to see the woman's face, but it was clouded by the morning mist. Startled out of his reverie by a ringing telephone, he jump up in bed and tried to focus his eyes. "Hello," he answered.

"Oh, I'm sorry, I dialed a wrong number," a child's voice said and the line clicked as she hung up.

Larry fell back across the bed and closed his eyes, things were just moving too fast. Most of his dreams were forgotten once he was awake and only a fuzzy remembrance would come up every now and then. This dream was different because every detail stayed in his mind all day long. He could even remember the scent of pine forestland and hear the sound of the rushing waters. He thought the reason was because it left so many questions in his mind. Of course he was involved in the surrogate mother search and naturally children would be on his mind, but how could he explain the angelic little girl?

The baby he and Christine lost was a boy. This thought led him to reexamine the little boy in his dream who still seemed to look like someone he knew. The boy was much too old to be their son that died. Then there was in his dream a woman whose face he was not allowed to see.

Still the dream had a heavenly ambiance. Was God trying some sort of divine intervention by putting the children in his mind. If so, how should he react? Surely not with disdain for the children were enchantingly beautiful.

Larry's mind struggled with the dream's meaning until he was frustrated and decided to put it in the back of his mind. Anyway, it was only a childish dream, probably the result of his searching. The dream's effect persisted.

CHAPTER 11

▼

Larry played catch-up with his business the next two weeks by going to Burnsville and Spruce Pine, North Carolina and making calls in Southern Tennessee in and close to Chattanooga.

He was glad when he arrived back home in Flat Rock. In his mail was an envelope from Samuel Simmons Associates and inside the envelope was a single slip of paper from a Miss Wanda Reemer with a Greenville, South Carolina phone number. A notice at the bottom of the paper read, "Please call after four p.m."

Larry called after six p.m. and a small girl's voice answered, "Hello."

"Hello, this is Larry Foster from North Carolina. I placed the ad in the newspaper."

"Hello, Mister Foster. I think I'm glad I answered the ad," the small voice said reluctantly.

"Then you are Wanda Reemer?" he asked.

"Yes, sir—just me at this number. I live alone, but I have close neighbors," she added as a precautionary measure.

Larry had first thought the voice belonged to a child—perhaps a daughter. "Your voice sounded so youthful that I thought you might be Wanda's daughter. You are over twenty-one, aren't you?" He tried to phrase his words as delicately as possible.

"Yes, sir, I'm twenty-three," Wanda said timidly.

"Wanda, I live in Flat Rock, North Carolina, less than an hour from Greenville. Would you have dinner with me and we can talk," Larry said.

"That would be okay." Wanda paused, "But I work in Greer and don't get off until three."

"Do you have a favorite restaurant?" Larry asked. "You did say that you live in Greenville," he asked, thinking he may have been mistaken about the location of her residence.

"Yes, sir. I mean … no, sir." There was a faint hint of joviality in her voice. "No, sir, I don't have a favorite restaurant—and, yes, sir, I do live in Greenville," she said with a nervous laugh.

"Good, we've got that straight," he teased. "How about the Red Lobster on Wade Hampton Boulevard?"

"I'd like that fine," Wanda replied.

"Is three-thirty … four o'clock okay?" Larry asked.

"Yes, Mister Foster. I can be there then," Wanda said.

"Good. That will be after the lunch crowd and before dinner. It will give us time to talk," he explained.

"Yes, sir, I'll be there," Wanda promised.

"Give the receptionist your name and ask for me. I'll try and get there first," Larry instructed.

"Thank you …" Wanda paused, "and …"

"Is something wrong?" he asked.

"No, sir, your name slipped my mind," she said hesitantly.

"Larry Foster. If you forget I'll probably be the only old man there waiting for a Miss Wanda Reemer," he chuckled.

"I feel so embarrassed," Wanda said.

"Don't. It just proves that you've got a lot of things on your mind." Larry spoke softly with sincere feelings for he seemed to denote a lot of sadness in the young girl's voice. "Are you all right?" he asked.

"Yes, sir, I'm fine," she answered.

"Then it's a date. I'll see you around four o'clock tomorrow at the Red Lobster on Wade Hampton Boulevard," and started to hang up the telephone.

"Oh, Mister Foster?"

"Yes …" Larry answered.

"Please keep our meeting secret," her wavering voice requested.

"I will, I promise," Larry vowed and said, "Bye."

✳   ✳   ✳   ✳

All evening Larry tried to put together the reasoning behind his conversation with Wanda Reemer. First, there was her age. Why would so young a girl want to mother a child? She sounded rational for she asked that their relationship be kept secret.

Then there was her aloneness which he supposed meant there was no husband. A twenty-three-year-old girl living alone and unmarried was puzzling. Maybe she needed money desperately enough to carry a child for nine months. could be aged parents, he thought, that needed money. That didn't make sense for her parents should be in their forties, younger than himself.

To him there was no clear or simple answers to Wanda Reemer, so he turned off the television and tried to sleep.

*   *   *   *

Larry stopped in Flat Rock and got the local *Times-News* before starting down the mountains. He loved the scenic United States Highway 25. Going into Greenville's northern side on Asheville Highway he turned left on 191. Approximately another mile on 191 he turned left on Wade Hampton Boulevard and there was the Red Lobster on the right.

"My name is Larry Foster. A young lady didn't beat me, did she?" he looked at his watch as he asked the receptionist.

"No, sir, we've haven't had anyone asking for a Mister Foster," she answered.

"Good, I wanted to get here first. could you please give me a private booth in the back where we can talk? And, please direct her there when she arrives."

"Follow me," she said. When she reached the last booth in the back she turned asked, "Is this satisfactory?" A look in her eyes told Larry that she suspected he was having a clandestine meeting with a young woman.

"Yes," Larry answered.

Again he checked the time. He was a good fifteen minutes early. He played a game of counting guests—the obese versus the slender. The obese had a large lead when a timid voice said, "Mister Foster?"

Larry quickly straightened himself in the booth, "Yes, you're Wanda Reemer. How are you?"

"I'm fine, a little tired. It's been a long day, but I can rest now. I hope I didn't keep you waiting long."

"No, Wanda, you're on time," he said as he reached out his hand

Her hand was limp and moist. Her looks were like her appearance—dull. Wanda's hair was a plain light brown and her eyes lifeless. Even her dress was an off-color of brown. She wore hardly any makeup, but he reasoned she had come from work and did not have a chance to dress up.

After they had ordered Larry leaned back and said, "Tell me all about your-self."

"There's not much to tell. I was wondering about you." Her question sur-prised him.

"There's a lot to tell about me. What would you like to know?" he asked light-hearted.

"Where's your wife? I expected to see a couple. This is all about a baby, isn't it?" Wanda asked.

"Of course you expected to see a couple. How stupid of me," Larry said. "I'm a widower."

"Your wife is dead?" She was surprised, thinking his wife could be sick and he had to come without her.

"Yes, Christine has been gone for some time," Larry answered.

"And ... you're by yourself?" she queried.

"That's right. I'm by myself and very lonely," Larry said calmly.

"You want a child to raise all by yourself?" The thought seemed unbelievable to Wanda.

"Yes, as I said—I'm lonely," Larry repeated.

Wanda looked at him with eyes that took on a look of sadness. "I'm sorry to be so nosy. It just seems ... kinda different," she paused briefly, Ato see a man wanting a baby. Seems to me that most men would be out looking for a wife," Wanda explained.

"I don't want a wife. I'm still in love with Christine," he said.

"It's still unusual," Wanda shrugged her shoulders, as if trying to hide her curiosity.

Larry thought he detected a northern accent as they made small talk during dinner. "You haven't lived in Greenville all your life?" he asked.

"No, sir, I'm from Boston. My parents still live there," Wanda answered.

He smiled, saying, "I thought I heard some up-north accent. How did you happen to come south? A young man?" he guessed.

Wanda looked down, twisting the red napkin with her fingers. "It's kinda per-sonal, Mister Foster," she said in a hushed tone of voice.

"I'm sorry, I didn't mean to pry." As he was talking he could see tears welling. He was afraid to say more for the silence was embarrassing. Finally he reached over the table and gently touched her hand, trying to give solace to the young girl. His sympathy made things worse.

"Why couldn't you have a wife?" she sobbed.

"What has that to do with you?" he spoke gently. "I don't understand," he continued.

"It just does," Wanda said as she wiped her eyes and blew her nose.

"All evening long, after our initial conversation, I tried to figure out why a young girl would want to be a surrogate mother. Do you need money?" he questioned.

"No, sir," she answered, looking down at her hands.

He leaned over to speak low. "And what does my being a widower have to do with your wanting to be a surrogate mother?" he asked directly.

"I'm sorry, Mister Foster. You came all the way down from the mountains and deserve more than just tears," Wanda said, trying to regain her composure.

"That's all right, Wanda. It's been a long time since a young pretty girl cried over me," he teased, trying to brighten their conversation.

"I'm not pretty," she said.

"You could be," he paused.

"I'm hiding, Mister Foster," she cried out.

"From your boyfriend … your parents?" Larry couldn't understand her logic.

"From myself," Wanda muttered.

"Yourself? You're hiding from yourself?" he asked. "That sounds like a mental problem."

"Yes, Mister Foster. It's as if I'm in a deep hole and don't have the energy or the will to lift myself out," Wanda said in a monotone voice.

Larry searched his mind for the right words. "Why … why are you in a hole? Why can't you get out?" he whispered.

"Will there be anything else … dessert?" the waitress interrupted, holding the check in her hand.

"Wanda, want dessert?" he asked and she shook her head no. "Nothing, thank you, waitress. We appreciate your fine service." He took the check and handed her a ten dollar bill. "Is it alright if we stay longer?" he asked and looked at Wanda to see if she wanted to leave.

"Y'all stay as long as you wish," the waitress said and smiled.

Larry waited until the waitress was beyond hearing and looked at Wanda, "We were talking about your deep hole. Who put you in the hole?" he asked.

"I put myself there," Wanda said.

"I don't understand," Larry exclaimed.

She spoke with glum, "You won't tell?"

"Never. I've already promised. Besides, what possible motive would I have to disclose our personal conversations?" he assured her.

"Mister Foster, you think I came to South Carolina chasing a boyfriend. That's not true. I came down here to get rid of a baby," she whispered as if her words were obscene and detestable.

"An abortion ... or adoption?" he whispered back, wanting her to know that he would support her confidence.

"An abortion." Her lower lip trembled. "Oh, I"m so ashamed," she sobbed.

"You can't forget?" Larry touched her arm in a supportive gesture.

"I can't look at a baby without thinking of the awful thing I did," Wanda picked up her napkin to wipe her nose.

For a while neither spoke. He looked beyond Wanda in an attempt to curb his own tears. "I can understand your regret for your action, but you can't undo it by punishing yourself," he said, trying to be comforting. "And you haven't answered my question. What does my not having a wife have to do with it?"

Wanda looked at him through her tears. "I thought that giving a child to a childless couple with a happy home would make up for the baby I killed," she sobbed.

Larry shook his head sorrowing, "No, Wanda, that only makes matters worse. Things don't work that way," Larry assured her.

"What do you mean?" Wanda wiped her eyes.

"Look at it this way. One baby is dead. Another baby lives its life wondering where its blood mother is and why she didn't want him, or her. You see, you have compounded the situation," he said convinced. After saying that he realized that he was debauching his own search for a baby. He felt confused.

The tears started again, "But how can I ... what can I do for I can't live with my guilt."

"Wanda, nothing can be gained by blaming yourself. The Lord knows your heart, you have a kind, loving heart because you care. You could never abort another child," he said reassuringly.

"Never," Wanda sobbed.

"Then get on with life. Fix yourself up, be happy, find a good caring husband, have children, live, but don't destroy your child's face. Someday you will know in your heart that you are a better mother because of the action you can't recall."

Wanda carefully dabbed at her eyes, "How do I do that, Mister Foster? How do I begin?" she asked.

"Go to church, develop a deep faith. And, in the process, fix yourself up."

"How can I fix myself differently?" Wanda's face reflected her perplexity.

"Go to a beauty parlor, get a new hair do. Put some color in that dull brown hair." He paused, fearing that he had gone too far, but Wanda's face said otherwise. "Get a cosmetologist and have her show you how to put on makeup. You'd be surprised to see what a little color to your cheeks and lips can do to put back a sparkle in your eyes."

Wanda laughed.

"And, for goodness sake, wear some colorful form-fitting clothes," Larry smiled.

"Thank you, Mister Foster, thank you," she said honestly.

"Will you let me know how things go?" he asked.

"Sure, if you give me your address," Wanda promised.

*   *   *   *

The ride up the mountains were fraught with discernment. He had descended the mountains to find a surrogate mother and wound up sending his prospect in another, more dutiful direction, but he felt good about his advice to Wanda. Again the thought that his search might be within himself came to mind. Was he inwardly feeling pangs of regret as far as his life with Christine was concerned? Certainly there were times he wished that he had treated her more kindly. He knew that there were many instances where he could have done things differently.

*   *   *   *

The next morning he awoke feeling depressed. He would never be able to get a child that he had fathered through a mother surrogate. Why was he putting up with women like Wanda, what was he going to get through such actions?

He lazily pushed himself out of bed. It was either go to the bathroom or wet the bed. While in the bathroom he looked out over the eastern sky. A rosy bright light was forcing itself to the edge of the skyline. The view and a brighter spirit began to venture into his consciousness. Would he ever hear from Wanda? If not, he had her phone number and would call her. With the thought came a smile.

CHAPTER 12

▼

Larry spent Monday morning doing his office work and answering business correspondence before he went to the pick up the mail. There was another lead, a Miss Corrie Shrum of Concord, North Carolina.

A little before two that afternoon he received a call from Sam Simmons. "How are you, my good friend?" Sam's voice sounded as though he was right in the room.

"Good, no complaints," Larry answered.

"I'll bet. Who wouldn't when you're out there interviewing all those gorgeous, anxious females," Sam laughed.

"You should laugh—not all gorgeous—not all anxious. Sometimes I feel like I'm doing volunteer work for the Salvation Army," Larry said, remembering Josie Moon and young Wanda.

"Well, they do a lot of charitable work, buddy, and we need a baby," Sam said optimistically. "The main reason for my call is that we received another lead in this morning's mail and knowing about the one from Concord, we figured you might want to follow-up on the one from Statesville."

"Right. I'm getting tired of I-85. This way I can go north and pick up I-40 east to Statesville and then go I-77 to Concord."

"Don't go down on I-85."

"Why not?" Larry asked, suspicious of Sam's way of thinking.

"Cause, buddy, I saved the best for last. This is really why I called. We had a drop-in," Sam answered proudly.

Larry was surprised, "A lead dropped in your office? Maybe before we get into that, give me the info on the Statesville lead."

"Oops, I'm getting ahead of myself. It's Lorna Tilson," Sam said and waited for Larry to write down the name and then gave him her phone number.

"Thanks, Sam. Now what's the great news about the drop-in?" Larry asked.

"Miss Jerri Jamerson, from right here in Spartanburg," Sam's voice filled with enthusiasm as he talked.

"Looks like I'll be leaving Concord on I-85 again. Is she anxious for an interview?"

"She's more interested in ten thousand dollars. Didn't say why she needs the money, but it must be serious. I told her that you'd have to approve any early payments," Sam said.

"Good. I'll try and be there around Friday if you'd like to give her a call," Larry said as he was marking the date in his calendar.

"We'll set up a meeting here in the office," Sam said. Then he added, "It's a good thing you haven't seen her or you might get a speeding ticket racing to get here. She's choice—big soulful brown eyes with dark brown curls glistening with auburn highlights. And what a body—with curves in all the right places …"

"That's enough," Larry interrupted. "We're talking about surrogate motherhood," Larry reminded his attorney.

"I know … I know. Sounds great, doesn't it? How I envy you, being single and being free to roam," Sam whistled softly.

"It would be great if I were looking for what you've got on your mind," Larry replied. "But I'm not."

"No harm in daydreaming—when you're stuck in an office all day," Sam said.

"I know," Larry acceded. "I've been there."

"Indeed … you're right," Sam said.

"My best advice is to realize that you never, never want to be a widower," Larry said slowly for it was a belief that he couldn't emphasize too strongly.

"I couldn't agree more," Sam said. "I'll let you go. Good hunting. I'll look forward to seeing you Friday."

Larry hung up the phone and called Lorna Tilson, wanting to be sure and set up a visit as soon as possible. This would give him time to make a business call on a fertilizer and feed plant in Statesville.

"Hello," a woman's voice said.

"Hello, this is Larry Foster. I'm the culprit that ran the ad for a surrogate mother," he joked. "Is this Lorna Tilson?"

"Thank you for calling so promptly, Mister Foster. It's Mrs. Lorna Tilson," she said.

"Excuse me, you see my attorney called from Spartanburg just a few minutes ago to give me your name. He didn't say Miss or Mrs.," Larry apologized.

"You don't need to apologize, Mister Foster, it happens all the time. I thank you for being so gracious. It will make things easier," Lorna said.

"Mrs. Tilson, I scheduled my time to be in Statesville Wednesday noon. I'd like for you to have lunch with me." Larry said.

"Around noon?" she asked.

"Yes, M'am. If we could talk then it would free me for business calls Wednesday afternoon," Larry explained.

"Will I have to dress?" Lorna asked.

"I think the Statesville sheriff might arrest you if you didn't," Larry teased.

Laughing, Lorna said, "I do believe you're right, Mister Foster."

"But—truthfully, don't dress-up. I'd like you to be comfortable. We could have lunch at the Holiday Inn. I think it's at Exit 21 off I-40," he said with uncertainty in his voice.

"It is. I live within walking distance," Lorna agreed.

"Then you know it's a traveler's stop-off. Women come dressed very casual complete with tired, frustrated husbands and raucous children," Larry said.

"Yes, Mister Foster, I know that," she chuckled. "What time should I meet you?" Lorna asked.

"I'll try and be there around twelve or twelve-thirty. If I'm gonna be late I'll call you. If I don't call I'll see you around noon," Larry promised.

"Thank you, Mister Foster, I'll be there," Lorna said and hung up the phone.

*   *   *   *

Larry rushed into the Holiday Inn in Statesville, not wanting to be late for his meeting with Lorna Tilson. "Good morning," he said to the lady at the door and then looked at his watch, "It's a little past noon, I'm behind time again. I'm to meet a Mrs. Lorna Tilson, I'm Larry Foster."

The lady smiled, "Good afternoon, Mister Foster. Mrs. Tilson is right behind you."

He turned to see Mrs. Tilson standing in front of a large leather maroon-colored couch. "Good afternoon, Mister Foster."

"I'm sorry that I wasn't earlier," Larry said.

Lorna Tilson did not look as he expected. Instead of a short brunette, she was a tall, big-boned woman with highlighted sandy hair draped fashionably, curling around her slender neck and gently resting on her shoulders. Her hazel eyes sparkled.

"Did I keep you long?" Larry added.

"Not at all. And, you aren't late, it's only twelve-twenty," Lorna said, not wanting him to feel uneasy.

"I'm not usually a tardy-type person. In fact, I wanted to get here early. I do believe they've increased the distance between Hickory and Statesville," he said, making up an excuse.

"Wait until you're fifty—they tell me that life really goes faster," Lorna smiled.

"That's it, I'm past fifty," Larry declared.

Lorna looked shocked in that she assumed him to be younger, "You're NOT!" she gasped. "I had no idea."

"Thank you," Larry smiled. "I sure feel it at times." He nodded his head thoughtfully. "Why you could get into trouble from a gaff like that—a strange man might take you to lunch." Larry smiled and escorted her to the dining room.

"Hide us in the back," Larry instructed the receptionist, "and if her husband shows up, don't tell him where we are," Larry teased.

"And he just might," Lorna tried not to smile.

After they were seated Larry said, "Better watch it, I've been known to bring tears to eyes much younger than yours." He was thinking of young Wanda Reemer and their meeting at the Red Lobster in Greenville.

His statement didn't bother Lorna. "That's no accomplishment. I've been known to cry just knowing I'll have to stick on my diet," she joked and added, "They make delicious luncheon salads here."

"Thank you," the waitress said as she waited for their order.

Larry waited for Lorna to complete her order and said, "I'll have the same," as the waitress was waiting he added, "We'd like our coffee now." He knew that travelers from the North seemed to expect their coffee after the meal. No so with him. He wanted his coffee before, during and after the meal. In that he drank it black, it didn't add calories.

Lorna watched as the waitress poured their coffee. "Do you dread talking about our subject?"

"Surrogate motherhood? Not at all," Larry answered.

"Well, I do," Lorna said.

"You're uncomfortable, aren't you?" Larry asked.

"Yes, very, but not for reasons you think. I have babies very easy. I love being pregnant. I can eat anything I want and does it taste good," Lorna smiled, remembering.

Larry chuckled, "Then what is it that worries you?"

Lorna sighed heavily, "That I wouldn't be able to give the baby up." Reality had erased her smile.

"But I'll be the daddy. Everything will be done business-like—only in a hospital or a doctor's clinic. Samuel Simmons Associates will handle the entire contract. You won't even have to look at my ugly face," Larry grinned.

"I know that. You have a nice face and you'd make a good father. It's a shame your wife can't have children," Lorna said between bites of her salad.

"Thank you," Larry said.

Lorna touched her lips with her napkin lightly so as not to wipe off her lipstick. "The thought that I'd be giving a childless couple a baby is comforting," she said sincerely.

Larry looked up from his salad, "I don't have a wife."

Lorna looked at him in surprise, "You mean you're not married?"

"Not now." Larry stopped eating. He thought he had told her about Christine. "We had a child that died right after birth. Tried for more, but ... it didn't happen," he explained.

"So you go around interviewing while your wife stays home," Lorna stated.

Larry put down his fork. "I'm sorry I haven't told you. My wife Christine is dead," Larry explained.

Lorna looked shocked, "I'm so, so ... sorry," she said.

"Thank you," he said. "But let's talk about you. How old are your children?"

"My boy Josh is twelve and Laurel is ten," Lorna said. "Want to see their pictures?" she added.

"Yes, I would." Larry wiped his fingers so as not to smudge the pictures. "They're fine looking children. I'd feel honored to be the parent of both," he said proudly.

"Thank you, Mister Foster. These are only school pictures," Lorna seemed to apologize about the quality of the photos.

"Your husband has dark hair?" Larry asked, "And of medium height?"

Lorna looked at him puzzled, "How did you know?" she asked.

Larry smiled, "Because Josh looks like his mother. I surmised that Laurel, with her dark hair and eyes must take after her dad. And although she is only ten-years-old I don't think she will be tall like her mother."

"You're right, Jack is short and dark," Lorna agreed with Larry.

"And you're thirty—or younger …" Larry slipped the thought in, wanting to know Lorna's age.

"Thirty-one," she said, "and don't think I didn't notice how smoothly you slipped that observation into our conversation," she remarked.

"While I'm on a roll, maybe I can ask a few other personal questions," Larry grinned.

"Okay with me. A man of the world who would ask a woman her age—can ask anything," Lorna said, laying her fork down to ready herself.

"Why are you considering surrogate motherhood?" Larry asked.

Lorna looked at him intently, "For the children. Don't you know at Jack and my age, everything is for the children," Lorna exclaimed.

Larry looked worried. "Is something wrong with one of them?"

"Josh is hungry all the time," Lorna joked, "but that's not it. Jack and I know we're facing college tuitions for the two children. He works days, I work nights, but we can't seem to get ahead." Lorna took a deep breath, "I still have some child-bearing years left, so we figured if we could get a nest egg for the children's college we'd be ahead of the game."

"You must love them very much," Larry said.

"I do, but don't all parents?" Lorna folded her napkin and placed it neatly beside her plate. "Now it's my time to ask personal questions. Why is a single man searching for a surrogate instead of a wife to bear him children?" she asked, her eyes never wavering.

Larry raised his eyebrows and attempted a wry smile, "Because I'm still in love with Christine, because I'm pursuing our dream of having children—but most of all because I'm lonely," Larry said honestly.

"It would be cheaper to find a wife," Lorna said smugly.

"How would I be sure she could have children? And, could I be sure that :I wouldn't bore a young girl?" Larry waited for Lorna's reply. "Women my age don't have children."

"I see, you've thought this out. Have you considered the cost?" Lorna asked.

"Oh, yes. I've already put down a deposit for Simmons to operate under a contract. They will make the initial and final payment to the surrogate when the baby is delivered, as well as all expenses," Larry explained.

"What are you offering the surrogate?" Lorna asked.

"It depends on the prospective mother. The lawyers won't make an initial payment until there's a sure pregnancy with my sperm being the impregnator. It will have to be certain that I am the father. That's why it's important for this to be done with surrogate and her husband agreeing."

"You still haven't told me how much?" Lorna reiterated.

"It would depend on your negotiation for a contract with Simmons and Associates," Larry answered definitely.

Lorna leaned against the back of the booth. "Jack and I wouldn't consider doing it for less than fifty thousand," she said calmly.

"Sounds like a fair price to me," Larry said.

They walked to the desk, Larry paid the check and then they walked outside the motel entrance.

Lorna extended her hand, "Thank you for the entertaining conversation and delicious lunch."

"I'll be glad to drive you home," Larry offered.

"Thanks, but I need the exercise." Lorna pointed south, "I just live about half-way up that hill."

"Thank you for your company, I enjoyed it. It's a special day when I can have a lovely lady to lunch," Larry smiled.

"Will I be hearing from your lawyer?" she asked.

"Certainly," Larry answered.

He went to his parked car and watched Lorna walk up the slight hill's sidewalk. "A very impressive woman," he muttered.

CHAPTER 13

▼

That afternoon Larry made one of his business calls and spent the night at a Holiday Inn. He was fortunate to get the other call done by noon and then drove south toward Concord, North Carolina.

Along the way he kept thinking of Lorna Tilson. She seemed to be the most intelligent of all his interviews. Too, she was physically strong with naturally good health and attitude. Her offspring were normal. She and her husband were planning the program together for the benefit of all. That was good. The one thing that bothered him was that in the whole family being involved—all had a voice of dissent. Even one of her children could perhaps influence parents to abandon the idea of giving up their sibling.

As usual the ultimate answer turned back to him and how he would react to taking the baby. Lorna was shocked to find out that he had no wife, which meant that her baby would be reared by only one parent. This idea, too, could backfire. Then he would be faced with seeing a child of his seed being raised by a stranger. *If only I had the wisdom of Solomon*, he mused as he drove south.

Before making his call he went to the bathroom and then checked his watch for the time. *Hmm, it's after five-thirty. Corrie Kendall oughta be home by now,* Larry thought.

Carefully he dialed the number. A small voice answered, "Hello."

"Hello, this is Larry Foster. Is this Corrie? I put the ad in the paper for a surrogate mother."

"Yes, Mister Foster. I'm so glad that you called. I'm very anxious to get this thing started," she giggled.

"Good. Can we get together at the Holiday Inn lobby say … tomorrow morning?"

"How early?"

"Oh, around nine or ten o'clock? I'm spending the night in Charlotte with relatives. I'd hate to leave too early," he explained.

"No, Mister Foster, I can't do that."

"You can't?" he asked.

"No, sir, we're having exams tomorrow. My grades are bad enough without skipping classes and exams, but your voice sounds nice." She paused and Larry waited, thinking that she was going to say more. "Wouldn't that be something? My boyfriend would go ape if he saw me with another man," Corrie giggled.

"You're a student."

"Yes, I am, but not a very good one," Corrie replied.

"But how could you carry a baby?" Larry asked.

"Like everyone else. There's many pregnant students at the university," she said.

"The university at Charlotte?" Larry asked, for Helen and Jim lived on Rocky River Road just a short way from the university. "Perhaps we could meet somewhere tonight?" Larry asked.

"Nope, can't. I have plans for tonight," Corrie answered.

"Then I'll just have to interview you by phone," Larry said.

"Shoot," Corrie said. "I just love to talk with deep-voiced men. If my boyfriend calls, I might have to answer my call-waiting and tell him to hold on while I talk with my male friend. That would make him furious to wait while I talk to another man. What a blast," Corrie laughed.

"You seem to want to agitate your boyfriend?" Larry asked.

"Why do you think I want to have a baby?" she asked.

"That's what I was just going to ask you," Larry replied. He wasn't quite aware of which tree Corrie was flying from.

"Why, Mister Foster, I want to make him jealous," Corrie said.

"I hope he's not violent," Larry shivered.

"Some of the time. Do you know what he did?" Corrie's voice was penetrating.

"No, no, I don't—and at this point I'm not going to hazard a guess," Larry answered.

"He had one of those things—you know—those things men do when they don't want to have a baby. You know, when they have themselves cut down there."

Larry thought of circumcision, but that couldn't be it. He knew what she meant, but couldn't come up with the word. "Ah … ah … you mean …"

"A Viagra," Corrie said proudly.

"No, no, that's not it," Larry stammered. The more he thought, the more blank he became. "Not vicious …"

"Oh, yes it is," Corrie said excitedly. "It's an awfully vicious thing to do," she asserted.

Larry slapped his forehead at his inability to come up with the word—and then it came to him, "You're talking about a vasectomy."

"Yes, yes, that's it, a vicious vasectomy," Corrie agreed.

"Corrie, a vasectomy is not vicious, it's a very simple surgery," Larry explained.

She sounded angry, "The why he did it was vicious."

"Why did he do it?" Larry was trying to understand.

"Because he didn't want us to have a baby," Corrie sounded disgusted.

"And you want to be a surrogate mother because …? Larry's voice trailed as if he was anxious to hear her answer.

Corrie's voice was indignant, "To show him that I can have a baby without him."

"I think you both are going to extremes," Larry said.

"He is—I'm not," Corrie argued.

"You're sure that he had a vasectomy?" Larry was searching for a plausible answer.

Corrie acted insulted, "Mister Foster, I'll have you know that I'm not that kind of a girl, I didn't look."

"Of course not," Larry said without hesitation. "But I was thinking … nine months is a long time for a young girl to carry a baby just to get back at her boyfriend," Larry explained.

"I don't care, I'll show him if it takes forever," she said.

"You'll be a mother forever if you don't give up the baby," he pointed out.

"Yes, I'll have to give it up. I can't go to school and take care of a baby, too. "It's—it's too much," she reasoned.

Larry was having trouble holding the phone. Corrie's reasoning was exasperating. He felt that he was going in a never-ending circle. "Corrie, listen … please listen. Your boyfriend could be bluffing to keep you from hustling him for a baby. He could have made up the vasectomy as an excuse."

"No, Mister Foster, he's just plain mean," she was defiant.

"Then why do you want to marry him?" Larry was still trying to understand.

"I don't. Daddy would never approve," she replied.

"Daddy doesn't like your boyfriend?" Larry tried to give comprehension one more chance.

"Because we're in school," Corrie stated outright.

Larry finally found the right question, "Corrie, how old are you?"

"Just turned seventeen. This is my first year in college, but I'm a fast learner," Corrie assured him.

"Listen, you're not old enough to sign a contract," Larry said.

"I'm not?" she sounded shocked.

"No, I'm afraid not," Larry said.

"But I signed a contract for my dorm room," she sighed.

"Didn't your father co-sign?" Larry asked.

"Yeah, I guess you're right," Corrie agreed.

"Corrie, forget about having a baby now. You've got a lot of living to do before you plan on being a mother. A lot of things could happen," Larry advised.

"Such as?" she asked.

"You might get involved with another boyfriend, one who doesn't have a vasectomy," Larry hopefully suggested.

"Well, I can't discuss that right now. I think my boyfriend is on call-waiting," Corrie said and hung up the phone.

Larry shook his head as if that would knock out the haze from his telephone conversation with Corrie.

*   *   *   *

Larry dressed leisurely and ignored the continental breakfast at the motel. He wanted to have his omelette in the Waffle House in South Carolina.

Pam and the other waitress greeted him, "Good morning, Larry." By now they all knew his name.

"Good morning, pretty waitresses," he smiled. "If y'all know my name, can the sheriff be far behind?" he bantered.

"We won't call him until you've had your last breakfast," Pam said as she placed a cup of black coffee in front of one of her stations. "Are you having your usual?"

"Yes, dear, sweet, kind, and pretty Pam," he smiled. "A plain omelette and dry wheat toast—that means no butter," he added.

"I know what it means," Pam taunted him.

It was mid-morning and several waitresses went to the back to smoke. Pam sat down beside him in the booth, "You really do watch your weight, don't you?" she observed. "That's how you stay so trim?"

"I run when the sheriff is after me," he said in jest.

Pam looked at him intently, "You're a good man, go to church and live right," she said.

"I couldn't live without my faith. Just consider how mean I'd be if I didn't go to church," Larry answered in a light mood, but truly believed his words. "You seem to be in a somber mood, anything wrong?"

Pam left to pick up his order from the cook's station. Setting his breakfast in front of him she said, "Nothing more than usual. It's Ander. He's giving me more trouble. I was thinking how different my life would be if I had married a good man like you."

"What's he up to now?" Larry asked after sipping his coffee.

"Oh, just being Ander. You know I took out a restraining order and divorce papers to keep him from harming me or the children," Pam's voice was determined.

"Does that keeps him away?" Larry asked.

"Not from the telephone," Pam explained.

"He wants to come back to the family?" Larry asked seriously.

"No, that's never going to happen. He doesn't care about me or the boys. He's into this Alaska thing. He wants to go to Alaska and start a new life, but he's fighting the divorce," she said.

"What's holding him back?" Larry asked. "That is, if he doesn't care anything about his family?" Larry didn't understand Ander's thinking.

"Money. He wants money for beer and to go to Alaska."

"What happened to his job here?" Larry asked.

"He got fired for being drunk on the job. Everybody knows he's a drunk. That's why he wants to go to Alaska. And I don't want my boys growing up where everyone is talking about their daddy being a drunk."

"How much would it take to get him out of your hair?" Larry's voice was pensive.

"More than I've got." Pam raised her eyebrows and asked calmly, "You don't have an extra ten thousand on you?"

"He wants you to give him ten thousand dollars?" Larry asked in disbelief.

"Not exactly. He hinted that it would take money to get him settled in Alaska—and that we could easily get that much money out of our equity in the house," Pam said.

"But the court wouldn't allow that?" Larry reasoned.

"Not unless I agree," Pam answered with disgust.

Larry finished his breakfast while Pam attended to other diners. When she brought him a coffee refill he looked up at her and said lowly, "I know a law office in Spartanburg that's holding that kind of money for a surrogate mother to claim," he grinned.

Pam leaned close to him, her lips slightly parted and whispered, "No."

"Hmm ..." Larry said casually, "new perfume—I like it."

He left the Waffle House, but thoughts of Pam lingered. The least he could say for her was that she was a spunky brave little gal who, with four small children, fighting an abusively drunk.

CHAPTER 14

▼

Larry arrived at Samuel Simmons Associates in Spartanburg at eleven-thirty. "How's our roving interviewer?" Sam asked as he took Larry's hand.

"Bushed, it's been a long week," Larry said.

"Did you make any outstanding discoveries?

"You could say that. One girl too young—an air-head—another young and guilt-ridden, but another that might just be our answer," Larry said hopeful.

Becoming eager, Sam asked, "You want us to follow up and get the ball rolling?"

"Yes, the lead from Statesville—Mrs. Lorna Tilson." Larry handed him the slip of paper with Lorna's name and address on it.

"Good, I'm enthused that we've come this far."

"It hasn't been easy," Larry said in all honesty.

"You're right. There are many things to consider, but it's a start," Sam agreed. "I'm anxious for you to see this Jerri Jamerson—from right here in Spartanburg. She just walked right in off the street." Sam said with eagerness.

"What makes her so special?" Larry asked.

"Wait until you see her. Man, is she something! Wearing that red dress and with those dusky eyes and long dark hair," Sam said, his mouth open.

They decided to go to the next door cafe for coffee. While Sam was ordering a slender elegant woman entered the cafe and spoke briefly to the hostess who nodded in their direction. Larry watched the approaching voluptuous lady dressed in a royal blue sheath dress with a wide blue belt. An enormous gold buckle was the only adornment on the dress. When she neared their booth her eyes widened as she looked at Larry and then her mouth curved into a seductive smile. That smile was it—her eyes sparkled from inward happiness. They reminded him of Christine.

Hearing Larry's intake of breath Sam looked up and gulped as Larry rose from the booth. Flustered, Sam introduced his guests, "Mister Foster, this is Jerri Jamerson."

Sam looked at her, "I'm glad you're here. I've been telling Larry about you."

"It's a pleasure to meet you, Miss Jamerson," Larry said. "Won't you please join us?"

Sam hastily slid out from the booth, "Why don't y'all go ahead and get acquainted? I'll see you back at my office, Larry—take your time—no rush," he said as he swept the check from the table.

Before Larry could summon Betsy she was there with a cup and a fresh pot of coffee.

"Thank you," Jerri said to Betsy as she poured their coffee.

"It's good to meet you, Mister Foster," Jerri said vitality sparkling in her eyes.

"Call me Larry." He didn't know why but he felt like a school boy meeting a pretty girl for the first time.

Jerri opened her eyes wide and said, "Larry … but surely there has been some mistake. You couldn't be anywhere near fifty years of age."

Again Larry felt himself reacting like a school boy. Surely he wasn't blushing? "I can't believe it either, but old Father Time keeps ticking," Larry said, trying to be modest.

"I don't hold to that. You're only as old as you feel." She reached over and lightly squeezed his biceps and looked with eagerness into his eyes. "Mister Foster, ah … uh … Larry, you look young, very young," Jerri purred. She pulled out all the stops—first appealing to his youthful appearance, and then his vanity.

"Ah-hem," Larry cleared his throat, "we should be talking about you. You're evidently young, but old enough to bear children," he stated flatly.

"I think you're right, but I've never tried," Jerri responded.

"Well … so … do you have a husband?" He felt silly asking the question but clearly he must get back to a professional attitude.

"No," Jerri said softly and touched her lips with her tongue, "haven't tried that either."

"I have to ask your age," he said hesitantly.

"I'm over twenty-one," she answered and paused. "Is that what you wanted to know?"

Boyishly, Larry half-smiled, "Sure—that's fine. You're old enough to sign a contractual agreement. My wife, Christine didn't like giving out her age either," he recalled.

"Mister Foster ... Larry ... could we get to the money part?" Jerri asked.

"Yes, of course. If you are chosen, how much would you expect?" Larry asked.

"It's not really how much, the question is how soon can I get some money," she blurted out.

"Well, there are funds in the account designated for disbursements," he said hesitantly, remembering that Sam said all money negotiations should go through the law firm.

Jerri snatched her large purse from her side and fumbled for a tissue. Larry watched as she dabbed the corners of her eyes which took on a sensitive expression. "You see, Larry, it's not that I'm all that money hungry. I'm not ... no, I'm certainly not." She waited to see the effects of her words. "I've gotten myself in a terrible situation and I need a few thousand dollars as soon as possible." Jerri again dabbed at the corners of her eyes.

It hurt Larry to see a person with needs that a few thousand dollars would cure. "Well," he shrugged his shoulders and opened his palms in a consolatory gesture, "we certainly can do something about that."

"When, Larry ... oh, when?" Jerri asked desperately as she clung to his arm.

Larry paused, not knowing exactly what to say, "We can ... uh ... we can go back to Sam's office. I'll get him to give you a check. But you see, I'd like to know more about your situation." With a look of despair he said, "I hope it's not a member of your family or a loved one who needs an operation." He waited, then added dismally, "Or your mother about to lose her home?"

"What a very kind person you are," Jerri cooed, Aso sympathetic. And your low manly voice is so very ... soothing."

Larry pulled his tie, trying to loosen the knot, "You see, if the problem can be solved with money, that's trivial, not worth your distress." He felt that she was worrying needlessly. "But you didn't tell me your problem. I'll need to know if I'm to convince Sam to write a check," he explained further.

Jerri looked down at the table. There was a short period of heavy silence. "Well, I may as well confess," dabbing her eyes to be sure her mascara wasn't running. "I've done a terrible thing," appealing to Larry for sympathy.

"Just what?" Larry's eyes pleaded, wanting her to confide in him.

"I'm afraid that ... that ..."

"Yes—yes?" He held his breath, not knowing what to expect.

Jerri fumbled with the crumpled tissue, "I'm just a bit irresponsible with finances," she blotted her eyes again.

Larry's eyes radiated sympathy. "There are times in one's life that we all feel that way," he said.

"It's my credit card," Jerri confessed. "Why, I never realized that anything could climb as high—or so fast," Jerri's voice implored innocence.

Larry breathed a sigh of relief and reassured her, "Oh, that's nothing, it happens to the best of us."

"But Mister Foster … they've canceled my card. I can't buy anything. I need money fast," Jerri pleaded.

"What you need is a credit counselor," Larry suggested.

"But I can't be counseled without money. I've no money to pay my rent or anything." She beseeched him, "Don't you understand?".

Larry chuckled and nodded his head in a positive fashion. "It's only money. We can take care of that."

But his words did not stop Jerri's woe. "But Larry, what if I have to walk the streets at night?" she continued to wipe the corners of her eyes.

"That would be catastrophic," he said. "But that's not going to happen to you."

"And sleep on those hard cold benches in front of the First Baptist church," Jerri cried out, unwilling to be placated.

His words were fervent as Larry reached across the table, putting his hand on hers, "No, no, we'll talk to Sam and get you a check—I promise."

She looked up into his eyes and blinked, "You're an angel walking on earth. How I wish that there were more people like you."

Larry felt relieved to get her spirits back to normal. "Just dry your eyes and gain your composure, or else Sam may think I've abused you with all my questions."

Encouraged, she said, "Yes, Larry, I feel better, knowing that you will make everything right."

Larry motioned for Betsy the waitress.

"Yes, sir?" Betsy asked.

"We need a check for our coffee," he said.

"Mister Simmons has already paid for it," Betsy explained.

"Fine," Larry said. As he started to put his wallet back into his coat he took out a ten dollar bill, "Here's something for letting us use your booth all this time."

"No, sir, he gave me a tip, too," Betsy declined.

Larry was determined to give her something. "Thanks for the booth, we've been here a long time," he explained, "and we've kept you from other customers."

"It hasn't been that busy, Mister Foster," Betsy said politely.

"Okay, then take it to salve my conscience," he said.

"Well," Betsy hesitated, "thank you, sir," she said as accepted the bill.

"Oh, you're such a gentleman," Jerri said as she noticed the thickness of his wallet.

Larry checked the booth to be sure that no papers had been forgotten, then asked, "Are we ready to go?"

Jerri took a deep breath and reached for her water glass. "I suppose," she said, blotting daintily at the corners of her brightened lips, "we're back to the real world where money-hungry demons take your money."

Larry waited and watched as Jerri stood, tugged at her dress and wriggled to smooth out the wrinkles in the rich cloth. Whatever Jerri's problem, she had excellent taste in clothes. *That dress doesn't look like poverty*, he thought. In retrospect, Christine would have loved that dress.

Jerri clung to his arm and looked up at him adoringly as they left the cafe. Larry smiled a bit bashfully because he was not accustomed to public displays of fondness. When they reached the Samuel Simmons Associate offices Larry held the door and with a charming look Jerri walked into the law office.

Susan gave Jerri a curious glance as Larry said, "Would you kindly tell Sam we are here?"

"Yes, sir, Mister Foster," Susan said as she pressed Sam's button, "Mister Foster is here to see you."

"Is Miss Jamerson with him?" Sam's voice asked.

"Yes, indeed," Susan said with a hint of coolness. She continued watching Jerri as they walked past her desk, then she dialed a number.

*   *   *   *

"My what a fine looking couple you make," Sam said with enthusiasm.

"You say the nicest things," Jerri smiled, flashing a wide smile.

Larry forced a timid grin as he held a chair for Jerri. Inwardly he wished Sam would slow down on the rhetoric for he was looking for a surrogate mother, not a wife. "We've been discussing some way that Jerri can have an advance check," Larry said.

Confused, Sam took off his glasses and looked at Larry, "You mean before the pregnancy is proved?"

"Yes, you see Jerri is in a bit of financial bind," Larry said.

Perplexed, Sam shook his head no. "But that is out of the question—absolutely out of the question. There hasn't been a medical exam. Are you sure that she's the one you want? I've been reading your report on Mrs. Lorna Tilson and I thought you had settled on her. Are you sure?"

Larry blinked his eyes in bewilderment. It wasn't his nature to make snap judgments. He had charitably wanted to help Jerri, not to decide on the mother of his child. He looked from Sam to Jerri, searching for the right words to end his vexation, "Well, I ... I ..."

Sam waited for Larry's words, while Jerri puffed her lips as if pouting. At that precise moment Susan burst into the room with a policeman following her.

"Susan, what is it?" Sam blurted out, not understanding his secretary's provocation in entering the room without being summoned.

Susan ignored her boss' question, glared fiercely at Jerri as she walked over to her and swiftly jerked the hair from Jerri's head. Jerri let out a scream and tried to grab the wig from Susan, but Susan was determined. She held the wig behind her and yelled, "Officer, arrest this fraud."

While all this was going on Larry and Sam watched in disbelief. Sam didn't get his answer from Larry and at this point Larry didn't intend to make it. Both men looked from Jerri to each other in total bewilderment.

"I am not a fraud!" Jerri screamed at Susan.

"You are a man and a fraud," Susan said solemnly. "Look at his biceps, his elbows. A woman's elbows come to her waistline, his go to the bottom of his rib cage. Officer take him into the restroom and check him out. I'll eat your hat, unboiled, if he's not a man—a fraud," she said, certain that she was right.

Jerri turned aside and said, "That won't be necessary, but you can't prove fraud. It's my word against his!" He pointed toward Larry.

The officer grinned as he blocked the doorway. "He's right, I don't need to check him—been there—done that," he chuckled. Then the officer spoke to Jerri, "Come along, Jerry, we've been through this before. This time you came out of your closet early."

Then he turned to Sam and explained. "Jerry Justice is well-known to the night crew. We've had to bring him in several times only this time he's working the day shift. Must be something important to bring him out so early," the officer said.

Enraged, Sam answered, "He was trying to get money."

"Did he get any?" the officer asked.

"Not from me," Sam looked at Larry.

"Nope, I didn't give her … uh … that is him … any money," Larry explained.

"Shall I give him back his wig?" Susan asked, still staring in disgust at Jerry.

"It's his, isn't it?" the officer asked.

"I guess." Susan hurled the wig at Jerry who quickly positioned it on his head and daintily adjusted it.

"I need a mirror," Jerry said as he felt the wig against his forehead.

"You need a head doctor," Susan retorted, her face red with anger.

"Do you want to press charges?" the officer asked Sam.

Sam looked at Larry questionably, "How about it, Larry?"

Larry raised his eyebrows, "Not me," he answered.

Sam turned to the officer, "I guess not. He can't do any more damage now that we know him."

Jerry's voice trembled as he asked, "May I go?"

"Yeah, you can go, but if I hear one more thing about you I'll run you in," the officer warned in a stern voice.

Jerry moved quickly toward the door and freedom. "Toodle-do," he smiled as he tugged at his wig and swished out the door.

"Thank you, officer," Sam said.

"It's all in a day's work," the officer scowled and followed Jerry out the door.

Sam and Larry crowded around Susan's desk, "How did you know?" they asked in unison.

Susan laughed, "I didn't at first. You see, you were always looking down at him, while I was always looking up. I could tell that IT was wearing a wig. Cancer patients wear wigs all the time, but IT didn't look sick and you heard what I said about the elbows. Over his two visits I became convinced. Had you listened carefully you could have spotted a voice break several times."

"Well, we're proud of you, Susan," Sam said as he patted her shoulder.

"Like the officer said, it's all in a day's work," she smiled.

*   *   *   *

There was a conscience conflict going on in Larry Foster's mind as he drove home. *How could I have let myself be taken in by a transvestite? I'm a man of the world!* he said, talking to himself. He remembered attending a show in New York City with a small group of men from R.J. Reynold's Tobacco Company where the entire cast were transvestites. But this he viewed from a distance and knew that they were men garbed in women's clothes.

However, today Jerri drank coffee with him and put her hands on him and the worst part was that Larry's vanity gladly accepted the puff of a transvestite. Was it his loneliness that compelled him to eat the plentiful dish of flattery? "Oh, well, how many men have been wooed by a fake beauty?" He laughed in an effort to put the escapade from his mind.

*   *   *   *

As Larry's car sped up the Saluda grade Larry smiled, thinking of the Jerri Jamerson affair. He crossed the Continental Divide, his spirits rising. Everything looked verdantly green, fresh and beautiful. His life seemed worth living.

CHAPTER 15

▼

Larry watched for Monday's mail because the factory had asked him to return to Darien, Georgia to wrap up an order with a chemical company. As always, it made sense to wait for the mail for other possible calls in lower South Carolina or Georgia. He didn't understand why, but the mail was always late when he was the most anxious to begin a trip.

In the mail there was a letter from Lorna Tilson forwarded from the Sam Simmons office in Spartanburg. Anxious, he opened the envelope and read:

Dear Mister Foster,

I'm sorry to have to write this letter but I must.

You remember my saying that we, my husband and I, were considering surrogate motherhood for our children's education. Well, Mister Foster, we have decided that we must refuse your offer for the same reason.

You see, we tried to look at it through the children's eyes—it was a revelation. Our children would see their parent's selling away their beloved brother, or sister, for money. You can see how dangerous it would be for us to put money above something which is part of our family. That, Mister Foster, is not what we want our ten and twelve-year-old children to see. It would look like a choice between love and money.

Please understand our reason for refusing. I did enjoy our visit and lunch. Thank you very much.

Yours truly,

Lorna Tilson

All the way down the mountain Lorna Tilson's letter disturbed him. Not that he thought her wrong, but that it forced him to look into his own heart. Of course, Lorna was right. He should have been the first to realize it. He had asked himself if either he or Lorna Tilson were mentally fit to be parents—but Lorna and her husband reasoned it out. Why hadn't he?

Arriving at this point in his reasoning Larry asked himself it there was any circumstance which would make surrogate motherhood moral. In New York City he had walked by blood banks and saw healthy and derelict persons go through its doors and wondered about their purposes for selling their blood. Was it for real needs or just another means to buy whiskey and drugs?

Again his thoughts turned inward. Were there any instances which would make his search morally right? Solomon would have flung his arms heavenward and shouted, "It's all futile—just chasing the wind." Larry asked himself, "Was his searching affecting others and their lives, creating lasting problems—perhaps creating chaotic discord? His answer was a serious strike at his conscience. Yet, if he and Lorna Tilson had gone through with the surrogate motherhood there would have been another soul on earth and who is to say what effect that soul would bring to others. As things now stand the Tilsons would not have another child to offend or enrich others. Where was logic, or the irony in the situation?

Better still, where was the truth as it related to him and his searching? He still hadn't confided his search to Reverend Evan Charles and he wasn't sure he ever would—at least not until after the fact. He grinned, thinking the reverend couldn't resist a tiny baby in its father's arms. Who could oppose it, or restrain its comeliness?

Then his conscience did a flip-flop. It was unlike him to be anything other than honest with his friend. True friendship did not connive, conceal or disguise itself from each other. He couldn't, or shouldn't, hide his intent from Evan.

Larry felt an urge to leave I-26 and tell Sam Simmons to stop the search, but that would cause problems for he had signed a contract which at the time had been in good faith.

Somehow the highway pulled him south beyond Spartanburg exits. At least life had taught him the hazards of making snap decisions. In Larry's conscience he was turning against his search for a surrogate mother. But the other side of his dilemma was loveless, the condition of his existence which sent him on the search.

There, in his imagination, was Hugh Mills shouting, "It's a damn lonely existence. Do something—anything—or you'll end up like me—just an eighty-year-old fart in the passing wind."

"But Hugh," Larry wanted to argue, "There are many alternatives to sitting in your rocking chair and complaining. You could became more active in church affairs—you could do volunteer work, or start a hobby like writing or art." Then Larry paused, "Or you could get married and begin life with a lonely someone like yourself." Larry stopped his insightful penetration for with Hugh he might make his partner his victim in rape.

Larry took the Waterboro, South Carolina exit and waited for the cars exiting Shoney's Restaurant to pass before entering the drive and parking. After visiting the restroom he waited for the hostess to seat him.

"How's this?" she said, showing him a booth in the far left corner of the dining room.

"Fine, thank you," he said, sliding into the booth. "I see a friend at the salad bar that I want to have join me." He was referring to George Jenkins, the man he was to call on. He quickly scooted to the other side of the booth so that he could watch most of the people going to and from the salad bar.

"Your waitress will be with you shortly," she spoke with a lowland South Carolina drawl.

He waited for the waitress to set down his lunch before leaving his booth. At the bar he tapped George on the shoulder and the man looked up. "Are you alone?" Larry asked.

"Yes, A George looked surprised.

"Join me, I'm sitting at that booth." Larry pointed toward the far corner.

George was grinning, "You white devil. You always show up at lunch time."

Larry grinned, "How's the system in Orangeburg doing?"

"Great," George answered.

And you need another one for the new plant?" Larry asked, for he felt this was the reason consolidated sent him inquiry.

"Yes, sir. I hope you've some spare time this afternoon," George said.

"I can spend the night here and go to Darien in the morning. That means, my friend, I can spend the entire afternoon with you. Besides, I'd like to see your new plant," Larry said.

"I remember something about you," George said as he stood up to go to the dessert bar.

Larry raised his eyebrows, "I hope it's good."

"Ain't bad. You were looking for a baby, right?"

"Yep, I was looking for a surrogate mother to have my baby for me," Larry explained.

"Did you find one?" George asked.

"Not exactly, but I've found some answers," Larry said.

"About that baby business. Did you decide on an older baby, say twenty-one years old?" George wisecracked.

"Nope, I ran into my conscience," Larry said. "I had a girl selected, but she back out."

"Are you going to keep trying?" George asked.

"I ... I really don't know. I've got to think things out. Surely there must be someone who could benefit from a surrogacy pregnancy and enable me to get a baby. I really need to be objective and honest with my own feelings," Larry said.

"The trouble is you haven't been looking for a black baby," George said.

Larry didn't know if George was teasing or not but he took the jovial path. "Somehow I knew you would say that."

When they had finished their coffee George said, "Follow me to the plant. It's a few miles southeast, you just stay with me. I've got a whole afternoon that will keep that black baby off your mind," he cut his eyes at Larry and grinned.

Their being friends and the success of the Orangeburg installation made the present job easier. "How soon do you want this?" Larry ask as he scribbled notes on his sketching board.

"Like yesterday ..." George was serious.

"Good!" Larry exclaimed.

Getting all the specifications for the new installment did take all afternoon.

✳   ✳   ✳   ✳

Larry spent the night at a motel near the interstate. The following morning he checked out and drove homeward. The new day held promise. He had another order in his pocket and there would probably be another name from Sam Simmons waiting. He smiled as the miles passed in exciting hopes for tomorrow.

CHAPTER 16

— ▼ —

Larry thought of going by Sam Simmons' office on his way to meet Pam, but since he was late getting off the mountains postponed it until on his way home.

When he walked into the Waffle House Pam was busy talking to another waitress with her back was to him. He noticed how slim and young she looked, her hair brushed to a light sheen and her waist as slender as a high-school cheer-leader.

"Good morning," the waitresses called out in unison.

"Good morning," Larry answered.

Recognizing his voice Pam turned, looking up at the wall clock, "Right on time."

"When pretty girls tell me what to do, I do it," Larry stated with certainty.

"Always?" Pam whispered something to the other waitress, turned, and took Larry's arm, saying, "Let's go."

Puzzled, he asked, "Where to?"

"Your car." Then she whispered in his ear, "I don't want the girls to hear."

"But ... but I haven't had breakfast," Larry protested.

"I thought you always do what pretty girls tell you to do." She spun around and raised her eyebrows, "Are you insinuating that I'm not a pretty girl?"

Larry tried to think of a good come-back answer. "No—not at all. In fact, just the opposite." He relaxed and then added, "Remember, a hungry man is a savage beast."

"You're right there. But after you hear what I've got in mind you might lose your appetite." As Pam pulled him out the door the other waitresses whistled.

Larry opened the car door and tossed all his brochures into the back seat. After Pam was in he got behind the driver's seat and asked, "Where to?"

"Nowhere. Get your foot off the gas and turn off the ignition. I only want to talk in private," she said.

"Shoot," Larry said, putting the car keys back into his pocket.

Pam sighed, "I need money ... lots of money," she looked steadily at him.

"Has this something to do with surrogate motherhood?" he asked.

"Yes. It's the only way I can get money. Ander has ruined his and my credit and I couldn't borrow a dime if my life depended on it."

"He's out of your life now," Larry ventured to guess from what she had previously told him.

"No, he's a long way from being out of our lives. He has a court order to stay away from me and the kids, but he won't sign the divorce papers. He's dangerous. I can't sleep at nights, wondering if he'll call and hang up, or if he's parked outside, watching the house." Pam shuddered, "And what's to keep him from someday coming up to our car and saying, Boys, I'm your pa'. You know courts orders are only for a limited time?" she explained with a pained expression on her face.

"How does he relate to your desperate need for money?" Larry asked.

"He has this idea that if he can't see his family he'll go to Alaska and start a new life. I've got him where I want him if I only had money, A Pam lamented.

"He wants you to bankroll him and then he'll leave?" Larry asked, wanting to be sure he understood.

"He'll give me a divorce, sign away all rights to the children and never come back. And if that happens I'll change mine and the children's names back to my maiden name," Pam said firmly.

"How much is the worm wanting?" Larry asked.

"He mentioned ten thousand, but I think he'll go for less," Pam thought out loud.

Larry was definite, "I'd give him the ten if it would get him as far away as possible. You don't want to haggle with a drunk."

Exasperated, Pam opened her palms, "What's the difference in six or ten thousand when you don't have anything?"

"So you've decided to become a surrogate mother?" Larry asked.

She looked at him, "For you."

"Why for me?" he asked.

Pam laughed lightly, "Cause you're the only man I know who's looking for a surrogate and willing to pay," and then she looked at him, hopelessness in her eyes, "will you?"

"Yes," Larry agreed instantly.

"How much?" she asked, surprised that his answer was so quick.

Cautious, Larry said, "Ten thousand with one condition."

"That one condition scares me. I already said I'd be your surrogate," Pam said, thinking that Larry would ask something unreasonable, perhaps something that she could never do.

"Samuel Simmons Associates will draw up the contract for Ander to sign and the money must be paid to him through the law firm. Everything must go through them, because that way it's all legal."

Overwhelmed Pam said, "That's all?" not sure Larry's words were real.

"You do want it so that he'll give up all legal rights to the children? You're definite on that? You don't ever want him to see or be around them again?" He waited for her to answer.

"Absolutely," she answered as though her heart was unburdened.

"About the surrogacy …" Larry started to say

"I'm nervous about that," Pam said, "I've some reservations."

Larry looked down and saw her trembling hands. Feeling sorry for the young mother with so much responsibility on her small shoulders, he said, "You've nothing to fear."

"You realize that I have no experience with artificial insemination," she tried to sound cavalier.

"Probably be less hectic than you're imagination," Larry tried to lighten her their conversation. *After all*, he thought to himself, *the money could mean so much to her*.

"It has to be, especially after living with a drunk," she said.

Wanting to comfort her, he said, "There's nothing to worry about. The surrogacy examination won't be any more than a doctor's visit for a physical."

"How do you know?" Pam asked.

"I've seen it done up close," he said, bragging.

She gave him a strange look. After a brief hesitation she asked, "You're joking?"

"Nope, I even held her head," he declared it a broad grin.

"You are joking," Pam exclaimed.

"No, I'm not," he shook his head with resolution as he watched the bewilderment on her face. "I can even give you her reaction."

"I don't want to hear it," Pam put her hands up to her ears.

"She bowed her back and mooed," Larry said, trying to keep a straight face.

Disgusted, Pam said, "You dog, you had me believing you."

"Believe—it's true. I used to raise cattle," he explained.

"Really? You were a cowboy?" she asked.

"You could say that I was a cowboy, but I think of myself as a gentleman cattleman. It was a hobby," he explained.

Pam suddenly remembered her job, "Well, have we ironed everything out?" she asked, concerned as she saw two cars drive into the parking lot.

"One little thing," Larry said, "you don't have to do this."

"Yes I do, if I'm to get the money—and I want the money ... I need it," Pam exclaimed, her face reflecting her worry.

"That's not what I mean. You can have the money without going through another pregnancy," he said, looking directly into her eyes.

Pam looked at him in disbelief. "Are you trying to back out of our deal?" she moaned.

"No, no, I'm thinking of you." His voice was low and heartfelt. "I just don't want to do anything that might be harmful to your health."

As she opened the car door and they got out she looked over the car at him, "When it comes to having babies, I'm as healthy as a horse," she shouted over the noise of a truck on the highway.

"Not horses—cows—we were talking about cows," he said as he hurried to catch up with her.

"Is there no end to your insults?" Pam chided. "Now you're calling me a cow," she said, as she opened the restaurant's door.

Leaning out the car's window he asked, "When do you get off work?"

"Two o'clock," she answered.

"I'll pick you up then. Make arrangements with your babysitter."

"What for?" she asked.

"We're going to Spartanburg to make a deal to get Ander out of your hair," he answered.

*   *   *   *

Larry hurried his breakfast and drove on to Gastonia. First, he called Sam Simmons and made an appointment and then made his business call. That afternoon he was back at the Waffle House in Gaffney to pick up Pam. "Did you make arrangements with your babysitter?" he asked.

"I'm free till whenever," Pam answered. Without her waitress uniform she was dressed conservatively in a simple cut black sheath dress with a red rose embroidered on the left shoulder. Her petite stature looked exceptionally smart.

He gazed at her admiringly, "No one would ever mistake you for a mother of one—much less four."

Pam turned to him as they were entering I-85 South. "I'm not sure I understood you when you said that I didn't have to do this surrogate mother thing?"

"You don't," he said, surprised that he hadn't made his statement clear.

"You'll give me the money whether I do it or not? Yet I have to sign a contract with this lawyer?"

"If you sign a contract, you get inseminated and become pregnant with my child," Larry was serious.

Pam faced him, "And the alternative?"

"We get off at the next exit, find a coffee shop and I write you a check for ten thousand dollars."

"With no strings attached?"

"Remember the one condition that we still go through a lawyer with Ander before you give him the money and make sure that he signs a legal document that separates him permanently from you and the children."

"There's a hitch somewhere in all this," Pam shook her head in disbelief.

Larry cleared his throat, "No hitch. I believe that money is only good for what you can do with it. I am, by nature, very frugal. By spirit, very giving," he stated openly.

"Ten thousand dollars is a lot of dollars," she maintained.

"I'm sure it is to you." Larry smiled, "I am not a rich man in many way, but I'm happy to drive my old car. I'd never spend money on a new car at today's prices, it would go against my nature. My home is paid for. The Good Lord has given me more money than I'd ever want to spend on myself." He squinted against the afternoon's sun as he adjusted the sun visor, "Again—it would be against my nature ..."

"Still, we're not related and you don't know me that well," Pam said quietly as if in deep contemplation.

"You may be closer than you think," he teased, referring to their surrogate mother relationship, before getting serious. "Pam, sometimes I make more than that on one commission. Money is like beauty, it's in the eye of the beholder. The amount is insignificant to me and it means so much to you." He waited to be sure that she understood.

"It must be nice," Pam said, amazed that anyone could have that much money.

"Not near as nice as you feel if you can help someone with a real need," Larry said. Then he turned toward her, "What's it going to be? The lawyer's office or a coffee break?" he grinned, hoping to alleviate the tension in her mind.

"You're having fun in all this, aren't you?" She glared at him, "I've never gotten anything for nothing. Let's go to the lawyer's office, I aim to do my part. Besides I think you'd make some daddy—gentle and just a little bit mean." She looked at him cautiously out of the corner of her eyes, wanting to see his reaction.

They talked small talk until they parked in front of Samuel Simmons Associates. Before opening the car door he faced her and said seriously, "There's something you should know about me—you see, I have a conscience that I must live with."

"That's encouraging," Pam answered without a hint of a smile.

Larry pushed the sun visor back in place. "A few week's ago I interviewed a lady. She and her husband, wanting to build a nest egg for their children's education, agreed to becoming a surrogate mother. They had children, a boy and girl, ten and twelve years of age. I put her name into the lawyer's hands for processing. I really thought she'd make a wonderful surrogate." He took a deep breath.

"What changed your mind?" Pam asked.

"How do you know that I changed my mind?" he queried.

"You're talking to me," Pam said.

Larry smiled slightly. "I didn't change my mind. They did. They began searching the future and how excited the children would be to see the new life growing inside their mother. How thrilling to have a brother or sister at their age—but then to sell the baby to a stranger ..." Larry paused, "It was not the experience they wanted for their children." He continued solemnly, "I wouldn't want their children, or any other children, to face that trauma either," Larry said his voice filled with sincere emotion.

Pam looked at him, "You're getting around to my children, aren't you?"

He looked at her and admitted, "Yes, I don't think I should run rough-shod over other lives when the Lord gave me insight enough to know what's right and what's wrong."

"There's a difference in the children's ages, you know," she said. "Mine are much younger and without knowing a loving dad."

"Your oldest, Scott, will be six when the baby is born. I doubt the others will remember it. You could hide your pregnancy with loose clothing, not telling your children about your condition. I think you might even fool Scott, but there's always the possibility of a slip by your sister or a friend. You'd have to take them into your confidence, you couldn't fool everybody," Larry assured her.

"You've thought of everything, haven't you?" Pam asked.

"I'm a worrier—first class. I wouldn't knowingly do anything to hurt your boys," he said.

"I know that," she agreed with sincerity, "but the danger they face with him around is a lot greater than what we're planning. I just can't get out of the real threat without taking chances," she declared.

He rubbed his head, "Very well, I wanted you to understand all possible pit falls."

Larry touched her arm before locking the car doors, "You understand that Simmons will want you to come back with Ander and have him sign the legal documents. That way we'll have his signature on the check, plus the contract." Larry explained to Pam the process.

"Let's do it," she had made her decision.

$$* \qquad * \qquad * \qquad *$$

When they got to Pam's house she insisted that Larry go inside and meet her sister Loren.

"I'm pleased to meet you, Loren," Larry said, noticing the close resemblance between the sisters.

"It's my pleasure," Loren said. "Pam talks about you all the time," she said.

"Good or bad?" he bantered.

"Always good," Loren answered quickly, emphasizing the always.

Then the boys came up to him as Pam introduced them, "This is Scott," she said.

Larry took Scott's hand to shake, "Howdie, Scott."

Scott gave Larry's hand one quick yank, "I'm tough," he said.

"And this is Billy," Pam said as she pushed the youngster toward Larry.

Frowning, Billy asked, "Who you?"

Larry softly rubbed the tow-head and smiled.

"And this one, clinging to your legs, is Todd."

Larry picked him up into his arms.

"This is little Robby," Loren said, showing Larry the infant baby in her arms. Loren's six-year-old daughter Megan was standing behind her mother.

Larry smiled happily at the family scene which he felt was precious. "Say, gang, let's go out and eat."

"Yeah," Scott said, "McDonald's."

"French fies and tas-sup," Billy shouted.

"You don't want to take this crowd out," Pam objected.

"Yes, I do," Larry said with enthusiasm. "I'll have the time of my life."

Pam looked at Loren and Megan, "I've got to go fix something for the bear," Loren said. "You know how tired he is when he comes home, but Megan would like to go," she said, looking down at her daughter. Megan smiled and looked downward.

Larry was right. He did have the time of his life watching the children take over McDonald's and climb the jungle jack while much a Big Mac.

*   *   *   *

Driving home the quiet was unnerving. His conscience took over as he began a dialog with the face in the rear-view mirror. "Proud of yourself," the face asked.

"Not particularly," Larry answered.

"You knew that she wouldn't back out, didn't you?" the mirror accused.

"I did not," Larry said, as if he were insulted.

"Sure you did," the mirror argued. "You acted so self-sacrificing that Pam would be an ingrate to refuse you."

"It may have seemed that way to you, but I didn't plan it," Larry was trying to be honest with himself.

"Don't blame it on your sub-conscience!" the mirror mocked, as if anticipating Larry's excuse.

"I don't know what you mean," Larry tried to be honest.

"Don't give me that I don't understand' thing. You put a bandage on your conscience and your sub-conscience by being so pure and giving, by being sadistic, down-grading money and then uplifting the goodness of your soul by spending it on a good cause," the mirror said with disgust.

"It was a good cause. Her no-good husband was physically abusive and a danger to Pam and those adorable little boys," Larry argued.

"She said," the mirror countered. "You didn't talk to Ander," his conscience answered back.

"Pam's a good woman—and a good mother—she wouldn't lie about a thing like that," Larry debated.

"You hope …" the mirror challenged.

Angry, Larry said, "Now look here, what will the children grow up to be in an environment like that?"

"An environment like what?" the mirror blurted back.

"You know … a drunken alcoholic father—with a cringing fearful mother and four boys—helpless little boys. All we wanted was peace for her family," Larry shouted and shook his fist toward the mirror.

"That's not your concern," the mirror advised.

"It's everybody's concern," Larry declared. "I suppose that you would like me to stay in my own little world and do nothing." His intonation was adamant.

"Oh, you'll do something alright, you'll mettle with them little boys' lives, knowing that you helped drive their father away. Have you no conscience?" the mirror accused.

"If I didn't have a conscience I wouldn't be talking to you," Larry fumed.

"You know that children are very trusting. They need a father figure in their lives. Are you thinking that's you?" the mirror asked.

Defiant, Larry answered, "Of course not."

"Yeah, that's you all right. You'll drop by occasionally, take them to McDonald's, show them how fine and upstanding you are and they'll buy it. You know they will," the mirror said with sarcasm.

"Get off my back, find another case," Larry said as he shook his head. "I'm sick of this whole conversation." He refused to look at the mirror another time.

Larry pushed the 94.5 FM button on his car stereo, turned up the volume a notch and relaxed. Darkness was crowding out the daylight and the setting sun cast a luminous blending of gold and red in the western sky, making the sky line resemble a giant stage.

I'm just another player, he mumbled to himself.

CHAPTER 17

▼

Monday morning early Larry dialed a number and waited for someone to pick up the phone. "Hello, Marshall, Larry Foster," he said.

"Good morning, Mister Foster. What's on your mind?" Marshall asked.

"It's cluttered, Marshall, but I want to talk about my car. You recall when you checked the emergency brake and you said that it operated off a vacuum?"

"Yes, sir, that's true," Marshall agreed.

"Well, last week my cruise control would engage, but not hold and every time the speed would decelerate. Does the cruise control work off a vacuum also?" Larry asked.

"No, sir, afraid not," Marshall answered.

"Can you fix it?" Larry asked, hoping he'd not have to buy a new cruise control.

Marshall was confident, "Of course."

Relieved, Larry said, "That's what I wanted to hear. When?" He was afraid that Marshall would be swamped with business.

"Well, Mister Foster, I'm filled today, how about Tuesday afternoon?" Larry could hear Marshall shuffling papers.

"I'll see you around one o'clock," Larry said.

"Make it two," Marshall answered.

"Two it is," Larry hung up the phone.

*   *   *   *

Larry took his vitamins, made a cup of instant coffee and sat down at his built-in desk in the kitchen. His mind instantly turned to Pam and her promise to be his surrogate mother. His mind kept popping up questions, many of which he had no answers. He was in the deep end of the river and the current had swiftly brought him to this morning. He shook his head, thinking that the current had been too fast because today he was to pick up Pam Adcock and take her to a clinic in Spartanburg where she would be artificially inseminated with his sperm.

At two o'clock when Pam got off from work Larry was waiting for her in the parking lot

"Hi," Pam said as if nothing unusual was about to happen.

"Hi," Larry returned her greeting. "Are we ready to go?"

"If the car runs," she said, her eyes twinkling like a school girl going out on a date.

"Oh, it runs all right," Larry smiled.

He tried to keep his car in good running condition for it was a source of security for him in his business. As they merged into the I-85 traffic he accelerated and pushed on the cruise control which Marshall had just repaired. It worked. He turned to Pam, "Did everything happen as planned with your husband and the attorney?" he asked with caution.

"Everything. I got Ander sober enough to drive to the lawyer's office," she answered.

Anxious, Larry asked, "Did he sign the papers?"

"He did. Mister Simmons is filing for my divorce. Just think, I'm gonna be free from Ander Adcock. I can change my name back to my maiden name. Mister Simmons said he'd handle that, too," she said.

"I don't know your maiden name," Larry commented.

"Pearson—Pamela Pearson. Isn't that pretty?" she said, proud of her family name.

"Yes, it's very pretty," he agreed as he ran her name through his mind.

"But it won't be done till the divorce is final and I've delivered you a big baby boy," she laughed.

"I didn't say I wanted a boy," Larry said, his voice uncertain.

"Mister Foster, that's what you'll get, cause that's all I ever have," Pam said with surety.

Larry lifted his eyebrows, "Then it looks like I'm gonna be a father to a baby boy."

Pam looked at him, "You'll make a good father. And you like boys, don't you? Mine certainly like you," Pam exclaimed.

"I love the little fellows. Often I think of Scott trying to be the man of the house and Billy challenging him on every turn … and there comes quiet little Todd climbing up my leg, knowing I'd pick him up and hold him over all his brothers," Larry reminisced.

"Yeah, and before you know it little Robby will be jumping out of my arms, wanting to mix with the crowd," Pam said.

Larry looked at her in wonderment, "They're precious, aren't they?"

Pam smiled back at him and then reflected, "That's an understatement. They fight and squeal—they run and argue." She shook her head, "But then their freshly scrubbed faces, after their bath, makes them look like cherubs. And once in bed they reach out to touch your face with their chubby cherubic hands and say, I love you, Mommie.' What little angels." Pam's face was radiant.

"While we're on the subject, did Ander sign papers giving up all rights to the boys?" Larry asked.

"He did. He was so eager to get the money he promised that none of us would ever see him again," Pam answered, her eyes bright from the lifting of her worries.

"That's sad," Larry said.

"Not to me," Pam shook her head.

"I mean that his children meant so little to him—when they could have been the joy of his life," Larry explained.

"The bottle was the joy of Ander's life," Pam stated with certainty. "I don't want you to think that I'm heartless about Ander. It's hard to explain, but living with a drunk that is a threat to you and your kids, someone who is unpredictable and out of control is like living in hell. And there's nothing you can do with him or for him. I got the court orders, but pieces of paper won't stop a drunk and it won't get him sober either," Pam said with conviction. "That's why I'm glad to lose him," she said in a firm voice.

"I can see that things have been rough. Drunks are sure hard to reason with," Larry said.

Heavy-hearted, Pam said, "I never saw Ander sober enough to make conversation. But I do know one thing," she said, gazing out the window at the passing countryside.

"What's that?" Larry asked.

"If I ever get married it won't be for lust and the overwhelming idea of young love and romance. I'll be measuring things like sincerity of heart, giving of love, understanding and the freedom of friendship. These are things that will be vital to the children's development. Hey, maybe that's why the Lord gave me the kids; so I'd grow up and see the real qualities of life and living." Pam looked down at her hands as if her words were embarrassing.

Sensing her mood Larry reached over and touched her hand, "I think you've come a long way in self-understanding. You can't blame the young for being young, but understanding our mistakes of the past can prove to be a valuable asset for the future."

Larry turned to her when he parked beside the clinic's building, Pam laughed and said, "Oh, no. I think you're making a habit of doing this talk before we go in' thing."

"You're right," Larry said. "I guess I want to ease my conscience. Are you sure that you want to go ahead?" He peered deeply into her eyes as he waited for an answer.

Pam realized that it was his conscience, not hers, that was bothering him. Without looking away she softly lay her hand on his and declared, "Now more than ever."

Puzzled, he asked, "I don't understand, why now more than ever?"

Pam didn't retreat from her words, "Because the better I know you the more convinced I become that you'll make a wonderful father. I want to have a baby with your genes. I've tried the other … now I want something better," she smiled at her choice of words.

"That's a sweet thing to say, but I hope neither of us will ever regret our actions today." There was genuine respect in his voice.

"But I'm worried," Pam said as she innocently looked into his eyes.

"I am, too—worried about the results of what we're doing," he was being honest.

"Our worries are different. What if I'm unable to give up the baby, what then?" Pam's face was grave and her mind soared with doubt.

Larry didn't answer for a moment. "I guess that we'll just have to wait and see," he confessed, "I have no answer."

"But I'd pay you back. I would—every last penny," she exclaimed. Her eyes were frightened, fearful of the future.

Larry laughed, trying to ease her mood. "We'll just have to cross that bridge when we come to it," he said in jest.

✳   ✳   ✳   ✳

They entered the clinic and were placed in different rooms. He was given directions by the nurse and when he emerged the nurse said, "You'll have to wait awhile. We like to elevate the woman's hips afterward for a good hour."

Larry spent the time reading *Field and Stream*. After that he picked up a magazine on *Safari in Africa*. When Pam came out into the waiting room he asked, "How would you like to go on a safari?"

"A what?" Pam asked, not believing that he would bring up such an unrelated topic for discussion.

"You know, go to Africa and shoot wild animals—sounds good to me," he exclaimed.

Incredulous, she asked, "After what we've just done? How could you think of something like that?"

Larry grinned, "Maybe it's bringing out my masculinity. You know, track the dangerous animals—kill the savage beast."

"I'll never understand the male mind," Pam shook her head.

Putting up his hand Larry said profoundly, "No, no—women always understand the man. It's the man who doesn't understand the woman."

Pam made her point, "Then why do wandering husbands always use the excuse that his wife doesn't understand him?"

"You got me," he agreed. "I've never been privy to that sort of talk," he grinned as he opened the door for them to leave the clinic.

"Are we having our first fight?" she teased, walking through the door.

"I guess. You're winning the argument," Larry agreed.

✳   ✳   ✳   ✳

On their way back to Gaffney Larry asked, "Do you think it took?" He was almost afraid to ask the question for it wasn't a casual topic of conversation, but what had been done was not very casual either.

"Larry, with me it always takes. I'm the most fertile of all the Myrtles," Pam said, referring to the waitresses' teasing her whenever she was pregnant. "Fertile Myrtle," they would taunt in unison every time she had announced a pregnancy.

"But those pregnancies were not artificially inseminated," he said, reminding her that the situations were different.

"The doctors seemed to know what they were doing," she said.

"Yes, I think Sam Simmons has been in the business for years. He chooses the best doctors, but it's expensive to have several inseminations," he informed her.

"The procedure cost you money," Pam reminded him.

"Yes, it will cost me, but no need to fight against it with worry," he agreed. He had learned when he and Christine lost their baby that there was no reason to worry about money when health or life of a child is concerned.

*   *   *   *

He stopped the car in front of Pam's house and her screen door slammed. He looked up and there was Scott pointing at the car. Before Larry could blink Billy was pushing his way in front of his brother and Todd was pushing the screen door open. Pam's sister Loren came out with her daughter and baby Robby, everyone excited and in a party mood.

"Look, we have a welcoming committee," Larry said, smiling as he opened the car door for Pam.

All at once Scott and Billy began yelling, "Donald … Donald." Little Todd tried to join the yell but was drowned out by his older brothers.

"Are they calling me Donald?" Larry asked Pam.

"They associate you with McDonald's. They're hoping you'll take them to McDonald's again."

"Okay, you guys, it's a deal," Larry said as little Billy's face burst into a wide grin and his chubby little finger pointed at Larry.

Larry stood in front of the porch, looking at the face from his dream—it was Billy. All through the evening he seemed mesmerized with the thought.

"Are you all right?" Pam asked as she furrowed her eyebrows.

Larry realized his strange mood, "Sure, I was having some peculiar thoughts." He tried to smile, minimizing his actions.

She whispered in his ear, "You're not a daddy yet … and you can't back out."

Her perfume was light with a fruity essence and he could feel the warm breath of her whisper, "I know," he grinned.

Long after he left Pam and the boys the perplexity in his mind lingered. Again and again he tried to visualize Billy's face with the face in his dream. *I'm just trying to charge the imagery with my overactive imagination*, he told himself, trying to forget.

CHAPTER 18

▼

Larry Foster thought that he always dreamed. Whenever his eyelids closed and his breathing shifted into another gear, he was dreaming. He also realized that he only remembered them in the immediate wakening, didn't everybody? He did remember the fantasy dream of the ladyflies and the small girl and boy. He even recalled their facial features and that was the most unique, unusual dream of his life.

There was another thing about his dreams that was a puzzlement. It was something he longed for, but it had never happened. could it be that God was keeping him from the dream? Or could God hold it back, knowing that it would keep him in the past? Larry shook his head, disgusted with himself. No man completely knew the mind of God and here he was trying to figure out God. Perhaps God, knowing Larry's mind, would give him the thing he missed most—a dream with Christine? Since her leaving, never once had any of his dreams included Christine.

The night was cool with balmy breezes every now and then. A huge mellow moon hung low in the sky as if it were ready to burst and shower the earth with gold. They sat on the patio holding hands and gazing at the southern sky. Her face was turned from him, but he knew it was Christine. He was also aware that he was dreaming. His joy was overpowering.

"Isn't the night dreamy?" her soft voice whispered.

"Being with you is heavenly," he said and for him it was.

"Why don't we walk down to the twin bridges?" she suggested.

"Yeah, and wear ourselves out. The problem of walking down the hill is that we'll have to climb back up. That steep hill is no easy climb." Larry knew from experience. He had done logging on the steep hill, cutting up firewood for their open fireplace.

"Sissy," she jabbed at his ribs. "We can walk around the county road, it's not as steep."

"Okay, if you're going I'm going cause I'll not let go of your hand," he promised.

Together they walked down the county road to the side entrance in the bottom land and slowly meandered down the gravel lane as moonlight shafted through the giant white pine trees, causing spotted places on the pine needles.

When they reached the twin bridges they sat down on a thick bed of pine needles, watching the moon's sparkling reflection in the fast current of the stream.

"Darling," she said, laying her head light against his chest.

Larry knew it was Christine's way of opening a conversation. He paused, wondering what she was getting ready to say. "Yes," he said expectantly as he looked down trying to see her face. It was hidden under his arm.

"Darling," she repeated.

"You said that," Larry reminded her.

"But you are. You're my darling," she said with assurance.

"I'll always be your darling and you mine," his voice was firm, with a tender expression.

"That's what I wanted to say," she pushed at his ribs.

"That's one thing no one would ever deny," he chuckled. "With your slow talk you're definitely a Southern gal."

"But if something happened to me, would you marry again?"

He thought that she would raise her head, but she didn't. "Never," he said with conviction.

"But darling, that would mean that you didn't enjoy being married to me," she said with a pouting tone in her voice.

"No, it doesn't. It doesn't meant that at all," Larry objected. "It means that you are the love of my life. Our love will last me forever, it could never be replaced or duplicated." His voice cracked with emotion.

"No, darling, you're wrong. You would be limiting love."

He could feel her head as it nestled against his side. "But I love you with all my heart," his answer welled from within his soul.

"And I you. But love is like a well-spring deep within our soul." Her words were compelling, "Our spirit, our love, could never be limited to only one person."

He could feel his eyes welling, there seemed to be a lump in his throat as he tried to swallow. Closely he pressed her body against his chest. "Darling, I just couldn't. I couldn't ever abandon our love," his words staggered as he swallowed deep gulps of air.

"No, my dear, you don't understand. The well is full to overflowing," she said with softness in her voice.

"Not for anyone else," he insisted.

"But darling," she tried to explain again, "our love will always be. It will go on through eternity."

"That's what I'm saying," he objected.

"Yes, my dearest, but now my time is over I must go."

Before she could finish he stopped her, saying, "No, please, dear God, no, no ..." He felt as though his heart was being pulled form his body. He struggled for breath.

Her hands touched his cheek as a dark cloud passed over the moon. He wanted to see her face, to look into her eyes, but couldn't.

"Listen, darling, listen carefully," she said, emphasizing her words, "He has decided that I must go and you must stay. He has more plans for you—earthly plans," plans to share your love," she said.

"I don't want other plans, I want you," his words were imploring.

"His wisdom is perfect and beyond reproach. You'll see, dear and that's why I must go," she tried to calm him.

"Don't leave me, Christine, I'd rather have you than life," he begged.

"I must, darling, I must," she answered.

"Oh, dear God, what am I to do?" he prayed as he held her close.

Again she touched his face with her palms and kissed him in the dark shadows of the pine trees. "Please, my darling, let me go. Follow His will in your life. There's much joy ahead, you'll see," she said, her voice calm and assuring.

Suddenly he saw a man standing beside them dressed in translucent clothing. His eyes were piercing as if he could look through rock. Slowly the man reached out his hand and Christine took it.

"No, please ... no," Larry gasped. The man did not speak. Larry could feel her hand her hand slowly leaving his. "No, no ..." his voice echoed loudly throughout the bottom lowland, but he was all alone, all was silence. Frantically his feet tried to stand, the slippery pine needles made him slide. Again and again he struggled to get his feet under him and stand.

Larry awakened. His forehead was wet with perspiration and his feet kicking wildly under the sheet. He sat up out of breath. Darkness still ruled the outside and he could barely make out the tree tops silhouetted against the skyline. He searched the recesses of his mind about the dream, which wasn't hard for he remembered it because it was so realistic. He doubted that it was a dream, but he was in bed and not sitting on the bank of Mud creek.

Whatever the experience Larry was certain that it was of God. Introspective ideas began to form in his reasoning. They included several ideas which he had rejected. Was God trying to persuade him to change his ideas? Surely they couldn't be wrong. The thought shook his confidence in his judgment. Was his conception of love different than God's? He had to admit that he was fallible and perhaps he should be open to change. Christine compared love to an ever-gushing wellspring and said that he was limiting love and God's will in his life.

How long he pondered the dream he did not know. That it was an experience he would not forget was a surety. Too, it was a very personal experience and with a purpose. And the searching of his soul persisted.

Standing before his mirror to shave he saw the darkened circles under his eyes, "Where is my real life going?" he muttered under his breath.

CHAPTER 19

▼

The consequences of the insemination muddled Larry's mind. What had he done? How was he to act when talking to others, should he mention the surrogate business? He took the safe road and told no one, hoping that his anxiety would lessen. Instead of worrying he became emerged in work, following up on projects already quoted.

*   *   *   *

Larry decided to drive to the beach and spend some time, perhaps that would quell his soul's inner turmoil. On his way to the ocean he made a call in Rocky Mount, North Carolina. He spent the early afternoon hours there getting the specifications on an air conveying system for a local tobacco company.

It was late afternoon when he got back on I-95 and drove south. Again darkness caught him before he could reach Lumberton, North Carolina, but he refused to stop until he was at the Travel Lodge Motel. He had been there many times before and enjoyed jogging along the parallel road where all the traffic in the early morning was on I-95. The air was warm and invigorating relieving him of the bottled up tension in his mind.

After he had showered he leisurely drank coffee at the motel office and talked with the night clerk until the day clerk came in. "You ever go to Bitsy's Jewelry Shop?" Larry asked the fellow traveler.

"Where's that?" the man asked.

"At the corner of those shops at the shopping center just up the road," Larry pointed North.

Another traveler was having a continental breakfast said. "She's got some fine looking pieces. I sometimes go in and pick up something for the little woman," he added.

Larry checked out of the motel a few minutes before nine and was waiting when Bitsy opened her jewelry shop. He had told her about Christine on a previous visit.

"Mister Foster, what a nice surprise," she smiled and opened her arms for a hug in her gracious southern manner.

"I'm honored that a young southern gentleman would come to see me. Old friends are a special blessing," Bitsy added. "You come on in and we'll just steep up our teapot."

While she was filling the teapot, Larry looked over her counter of jewelry on display. "You've got a lot of pretty pieces," he said.

"Yes, we get them in regular shipments. My customers want new things," Bitsy said. "It's too bad you don't have anyone to buy gifts for," she said, remembering Christine's leaving.

A sheepish grin flooded his face, "Maybe I have."

Bitsy stopped and put down the teapot, "Really?" she asked, not quite believing what he was saying.

"Really," he agreed.

"She must be someone special," Bitsy said.

"She is," Larry said. He wanted to talk about Pam, but no way did he intend mentioning the insemination.

Bitsy clasped her hands together in grand fashion as she announced, "We must celebrate. I've some left-over banana bread. It will be lovely with my orange pekoe blend tea."

"Well, I can't hardly refuse that, can I?" he said as he seated himself at the small round table.

"Who is she? What is she like?" her voice raised in excitement.

"Pam's a waitress," Larry said, but he skirted around any mention of the children. "We're just good friends," he added.

"Are you planning on a gift?" Bitsy asked, thinking it would be nice to begin the day with an order.

"Something nice and simple," he said.

"I understand completely, surely I do," Bitsy drawled in her best congenial manner.

Before leaving, Larry bought a gold chain with matching earrings.

From Lumberton Larry kept on I-95 South to the Myrtle Beach exit, he checked into the Ship Ahoy Motel which was right on the beach and next door to a nice restaurant and pier. He stayed there for the remainder of the week. When he wasn't by the pool doing his paperwork he was swimming in the ocean or lying in the sun. Other times he lingered in the restaurant drinking coffee and enjoying small talk with the waitresses.

Saturday morning early he left for home.

* * * *

Every weekend Larry called consolidated Air Conveying Company to keep on top of the quotations in his territory, add new ones or to pick up any messages. If Sam Simmons was tell him that the insemination didn't take Larry would be asked to come back for another try, he reasoned, but the other possibility—a positive insemination—was too mind-boggling to imagine, its consequences too baffling. Nope, he just wasn't ready to consider that possibility and he forced his mind to think of other things.

Through Tennessee he went north to Charleston, West Virginia and north, calling on mining companies and factories throughout the river valleys. Finally he stopped running and headed south through Roanoke, Virginia to the North Carolina mountains and home. The first thing he checked was his answering machine. There was plenty on it, but nothing from Sam Simmons Associates, or nothing from Gaffney, South Carolina.

* * * *

On Sunday he spoke to Reverend Evan Charles after the morning worship service, but it was only a greeting because there was a long line of church people waiting to shake the pastor's hand. Evan was, as usual, very friendly, but there seemed to be a questioning expression on his face, or was it his imagination, Larry wondered.

Now the time of his self-exiled travels had come to an end, he told himself. Surely Pam would know whether or not the insemination took so he decided to plan a trip that would take him to where she worked. If it didn't and Pam wasn't pregnant he would go see Sam Simmons and cancel the contract. He shook his head and guessed that he was too old for situations like this. Sunday afternoon lagged on and on as he pondered what might or might not be. The night was no better so he got up early Monday morning and drove to Gaffney, South Carolina.

Pam was talking to another waitress when he walked into the Waffle House. "Good morning," the girls all called.

"Good morning," Larry answered the greeting in a weak voice, all the while looking at Pam. Her uniform was loose, especially around her waist and hips, but she was smiling with a special radiance on her face. Larry went to the end of the bar to his usual seat.

Pam followed him with a cup of steaming hot coffee. "Here's your coffee," and leaned over and whispered in his ear, "Daddy."

All Larry could do with his mouth wide open was to look at her eyes questionably which glistened like polished gems of aquamarine. She was smiling, her even white teeth nestled neatly behind her pink lips. Stunned, he gazed at her quizzically for what seemed like an eternity and he was frozen in space, unable to make human sounds.

Pam was close, still smiling, "You gonna have your usual?" Her voice came from a deep empty void.

"No, I've had breakfast," He heard himself saying—which was a lie.

"Is there anything I can get you?" she whispered, her face still radiant.

"Yes." Larry looked up, "Put this in a Styrofoam cup. I want to drink it in the car." He heard himself talking, but his words were coming from somewhere else

"I'll go with you," Pam said, filling a large cup with coffee and motioning to another waitress to mind her station. She knew that he was not behaving like himself and it concerned her.

Larry always locked the car. Now he couldn't get the key in the hole and fumbled nervously.

"Let me help you," Pam said, taking the car keys and holding his coffee.

Slowly Larry slid behind the driver's seat and pushed the unlock button for Pam to get in. A dark cloud seemed to hover over his head as he sipped the coffee.

"Are you all right?" Pam asked as her eyes searched his face.

Larry rubbed his forehead. "I really don't know," he said and then he asked, "did you call me Daddy?"

"Yes," her voice sounded light and bright and beautiful.

Larry straightened his shoulders, breathed deeply and laughed, trying to make a joke out of his overacting imagination, "That's good, I thought you were saying that you were pregnant."

"I am," she said, smiling as she looked into his eyes.

He gazed back at her to see if she meant it, "You're joking."

"Nope, I'm pregnant all right. Drink your coffee," Pam said.

Larry took a large gulp of the black brew, "And it's my ... I mean, I'm the daddy?" he was finally able to say.

"All yours, all documented by Samuel Simmons Associates," Pam said.

"Then it's certain? It's true?" His voice cracked and he sounded like a teenager whose voice was changing.

"Very. That's what you wanted, wasn't it?" she asked, her eyes searching his.

"Yes, yes." He looked at her, "When can I see it?" he said, without a hint of humor.

Pam laughed, "When it gets here ... in a little over five months," she said, not believing his reaction to the news.

To make sure that his reasoning prowess had returned he held up his left hand with his index finger outstretched. "And one will make five," he said, referring to the number of Pam's children.

"Are you happy?" she asked.

"I'm numb. How are the boys?" Larry asked, not knowing what to say or how he was supposed to react.

"They all have been asking for the Donald-man, I'm afraid that's your name now. But really, they've missed you. You've been gone for so long," she looked worried.

"Can you get off work?" he asked.

"What do you have in mind?" Pam answered.

"Taking the guys to McDonald's."

"I've got a job, remember? You go ahead without me, Daddy, I'll call Loren and tell her you're on your way." As she started back to work she turned and said, "Thanks for the necklace and earrings, they're lovely," she beamed.

"What necklace? What earrings?" he asked with a blank expression.

"These," she said, showing him the box. "You gave them to me when you first came in. I was looking at them when you decided to cast off from this planet."

He shook his head, still not believing.

CHAPTER 20

▼

Larry had been in Winston Salem, North Carolina for three days at the R.J. Reynolds Tobacco Company. He decided to go home through Charlotte and spend the night. Early morning he stopped by the Gaffney Waffle House.

"I've got good news," Pam said excitedly.

"What?" Larry answered.

"The baby's moving," Pam giggled and whispered in a low voice, not wanting anyone to hear.

"It has? But you still don't look pregnant." He was telling the truth, she didn't have a bulging stomach.

"Let's go over to the corner booth where we can talk," Pam said. Only two customers were in the Waffle House as they went to the farthest corner. "I was worried about the baby," Pam explained. "It wasn't placing itself like my other babies."

Frowning, Larry asked, "I don't understand, what do you mean?"

"All my other babies pushed against my waistline, but this baby boy is in my lower abdomen and was not moving. Naturally the baby, being it was conceived differently, well, I thought …" Pam wasn't sure how to express herself. "I just worried." She blinked her eyes.

"How long will it be?" Larry asked, trying to figure out the baby's due date.

Pam looked around as she was thinking, "Just a week short of three months, unless it's early." She figured, "And it could be early."

"Why do you say that?" he asked with a troubled expression on his face.

"Because this baby is different. I don't know if it's the new method or the new daddy, but this is nothing like my other pregnancies." Pam expression was definite.

He anxiously rushed his questions, "Is it harder to carry? Are you feeling sick?"

"No, not that. It's so easy that sometimes I scarcely know I'm pregnant. It's my easiest pregnancy and hard to believe. I really don't think I have to wear loose uniforms to hide it." She smiled as she patted her tummy as if to make sure the baby knew she was there.

Concerned, he said, "Good, my conscience is taking a beating as it is, I'd hate it if you were to get sick or something might go wrong." She could see a concerned look on his face.

"Why?" She looked at him with a pained expression.

"Because it's all my doing," he said full of self-incrimination.

"It's my doing," she corrected him.

"But you're doing it because of me. The idea seemed so simple and harmless at first ..." He turned his head, "But when you're effecting other lives it becomes serious—fast."

"No, I'll not let you take all the blame. It takes two to make a contract—with Samuel Simmons Associates in the middle." She was trying to lift his spirits—then she remembered Ander, "Don't forget, without you and Sam I'd still be fearing for my life and the children's safety. I'll always be grateful for that. I tell myself every day that no matter how things turn out—whatever happens—you were my way out." She touched his hand, "I'll always be beholden to you." He could tell that she meant her words by the expression on her face.

He raised his eyes to meet hers, "Thanks." And their talking reminded him of the children, "How's the boys?"

"Billy and Scott ask about Donald all the time. I'm not sure about Todd. He's saying something, but heaven knows what. When we mention you he goes into a talking frenzy and gobbles like a turkey," she laughed, thinking abut the little boy's jabbering.

"You'll be understanding him enough in a few more months," Larry grinned.

"He's already got his running game perfected, he races to catch up to his older brothers," Pam smiled.

"I wish that I could go see them," Larry expressed regrets, "but I've so much to do. I don't think I'll ever catch up. One thought further," Larry said, "you think this baby is a girl, don't you?"

Pam bit her lower lip softly before answering, "I think I do," she said hesitating. "It's either that, or a very small boy." She paused, "The doctor said that he thought it was a little girl, but it's too far-fetched to hope. One thing for sure, it's sweet. The boys kicked at my insides, but this baby acts as thought it's melting into its nest—even when it turns—it's gentle."

"You'd like to have a baby girl, wouldn't you?" Larry asked softly.

"I suppose, just to prove I could do it." There was a nostalgic expression on her face, then her eyes began welling, "After four boys I don't think that it's possible."

Concerned, Larry asked, "What's wrong?"

"Life is so cruel," Pam began rubbing her palms and looking down.

"Why do you say that?" he asked, unnerved by her tears.

"It gives me what I've always hoped for and then takes it away," she said, tears falling gently down her cheeks.

Larry knew what she was thinking. "It hasn't happened yet. Let's wait until it does, before worrying," he suggested as he reached across the table top and patted her hand.

Pam's words of denial didn't lessen Larry's feeling of being responsible for uprooting her life. He tried to reason as she did, but still he felt like his errant thoughts had gone too far. He should never have mentioned his innermost loneliness to Don Keeney, then he wouldn't have known Samuel Simmons Associates.

$$* \qquad * \qquad * \qquad *$$

Larry sat in the middle back pew Sunday, hoping to be the first to shake Pastor Evan Charles' hand and leave the service.

"It's good to see you this morning, Mister Foster," Evan smiled broadly.

"It's good to be here, Evan. I'm baking a chocolate cake this afternoon for my pastor if I can get him out to my house tomorrow," Larry said hastily for the people were lining up behind him.

"Can I have two slices?" Evan asked.

"What you don't eat you take home to Carolyn."

"What time?"

"Whatever suits you," Larry said, letting go of Evan's hand and moving to the side.

"Nine or ten," Evan said looking over someone's shoulder.

"The earlier the better," Larry answered.

✳   ✳   ✳   ✳

That afternoon Larry baked a double Dutch chocolate cake and put the two layers in the freezer. Early Monday morning he whipped up a soft butter, double chocolate icing and then took the frozen layers from the freezer. After icing the cake he topped it with mini-marshmallows, red and green maraschino cherries. Then he placed it on the kitchen table as a centerpiece, put out two dessert dishes, napkins, and two coffee mugs.

Reverend Evan Charles arrived a few minutes past ten o'clock morning, "I'm sorry, I just couldn't get away. The phone kept ringing every time I got to the door," Evan apologized.

"You're fine, I'll still give you your cake," Larry teased.

"And what a delicious looking cake it is," Evan exclaimed, licking his lips in anticipation. "My good friend, I'd like to share a thought with you," Evan said seriously. "You know that a lot of my job is counseling the flock?"

"Yes, I realize that," Larry agreed.

"And almost all the time it deals with death or tragedy with exploding emotions. I've learned that a little levity helps." His voice was serious, "In fact, it's vital to my survival at times."

With honest concern in his voice Larry said, "I know that and admire you for it."

"Good. Now, can I have my cake?" Evan asked as he rubbed his palms together.

Larry served his pastor a large slice and took a small slice for himself. "I'm not much of an eater when it comes to morning sweets," he explained.

"Good, more for me," Evan countered as he swallowed a large piece of the chocolate cake. "It's delicious," Evan murmured, picking up the napkin to wipe his mouth.

Larry raised his eyebrows. "Pastor, I need help."

"We all do," Evan remarked. "What have you been into now?"

"I don't know how to start," Larry said as he looked meekly at his friend. It was a topic he had no experience discussing, certainly not with a preacher.

"Start at the beginning," Evan said and added, Athat's basic to solving mysteries."

"Well, I didn't mean to be immoral or mess up anyone's life or anything like that," he stammered. "It was ... just one errant thought to a friend in Spartanburg … and before I knew it I had signed a contract with a law firm …" Larry shrugged his shoulders.

"That doesn't sound immoral, it sounds legal. It's that errant thought that jabs at my curiosity," Evan said as he pushed his plate to Larry for another slice of cake.

"I only mentioned how lonely I was to a friend. We talked about surrogate motherhood because I recently read an article on it in a Spartanburg newspaper. It seems to be an option for childless couples and South Carolina laws are open to this sort of thing," Larry said.

Evan looked up, "The plot is as thick as the icing on this cake," he observed.

Larry took a deep breath and said, "Before I realized what was happening Don, my friend, had made me an appointment with this law firm that specializes with surrogate mothers," Larry said. "And, without really considering the matter, I had signed a contract."

Evan put down his fork, "Have you gotten a woman pregnant by this process?" he asked with a serious face.

"Yes," Larry admitted. "Do you consider that immoral?" His eyes were large with a questioning expression.

"Not in itself. Sometimes it's necessary if there's an impediment in one or the other participants, if you know what I mean," Evan explained as he wiped his mouth.

"Yes, I know what you mean. I'm not impotent," Larry explained quickly.

"Neither are you married," Evan's voice was serious. "Is the woman participant married?" he asked.

"She was."

Reverend Charles Evans pushed his chair back from the table and folded his napkin. "Let's recoup. This woman who was married …" he kept staring at Larry, "and you have entered into a legal contract concerning surrogate motherhood. "m I right so far?" he leaned over toward Larry and waited for an answer.

"Yes," Larry agreed, "you're right."

Evan continued, "Now she's pregnant with your baby and you want to know if that's immoral?" He looked at Larry without blinking.

"Yes," Larry answered.

"Boy, have you come up with a doozy … and it's only Monday morning." He turned his head from side to side.

"It's legal," Larry asserted in a strong voice.

"But I don't think it's moral. Did it have anything to do with her marriage?" Evan asked.

"Yes." Larry wanted to be frank, "Actually it had everything to do with her husband leaving."

"You mean that you ran the woman's husband off and then pregnated his wife?" Evan queried.

"Well, Pastor, you're jumping to conclusions." He wanted to chuckle, but his pastor had a very serious expression on his face. "Please let me explain. She needed money to get rid of a drunken, abusive husband who was a physical threat to her and her children," Larry stated as a defense. "She and her children's lives were threatened."

"She has other children?" Evan asked.

"Four," Larry answered.

"And now she's pregnant with another one?" Evan asked, his eyes wild.

"With my sperm," Larry nodded with an innocent expression in his eyes.

"Are you going to take this baby?" Evan asked.

"I'm entitled to," Larry said, "it's in the contract," he explained with pride.

"Yes, but are you?" Evan insisted.

"I honestly don't know," Larry confessed.

Evan threw up his hands and again leaned back from the table. "You've really come up with a wild one. I deal in love relationships, not contracts. I believe you should chuck the whole thing and go back to the idea of getting a doggie," Evan shrugged his shoulders.

"I can't do that," Larry said.

"There's feelings involved, isn't there?" Evan surmised.

"Yes, definitely," Larry admitted. "You see, Pam has four boys and she's always wanted a girl. She thinks this baby is a girl," Larry told him.

"How old is she?" Evan gasped.

"Thirty," Larry answered.

Evan stared down at his empty plate. "She's sure been busy, and now there's about to be another—with no husband." Evan nodded his head.

"Pam's a waitress at a Waffle House," Larry said.

"She's truly a marvel," Evan smiled. "How are her boys?"

"They're great. Just as lovable as they can be. The oldest is five. He may be six by now, I'm not sure." Larry's eyes took on a warm light as he talked about the boys.

"Now we're getting somewhere," Evan smiled. "The solution is obvious."

"What?" Larry explained anxiously.

"Give the boys the dog and you take the mother ... I mean in marriage," Evan said the last part with a positive and proud voice.

"I can't," Larry said.

"Why not?" Evan queried.

"I still love Christine," Larry's face was solemn.

Evan straightened his back and admired the cake. "Don't offer me another piece. I want Carolyn to see how sinful your cooking is." Then he turned to Larry, "Was it Shakespeare who said ... *to thine own self be true*?"

"I think so," Larry agreed.

"What he meant in our present day English is be true to yourself. To do that we must know ourselves. Do you agree?" Evan asked.

"Yes, I suppose," Larry answered.

"My friend, you just said that you love Christine. Are you telling me that your love is so shallow that there's none left for anyone else?"

Larry waited pensively and said, "I may have said it, but I don't mean it."

"Good, I'm glad to hear that." Evan sighed, "I hate sounding like a preacher, but—we've all heard that the Lord moves in mysterious ways, remember?"

"Yes, I've heard it a million times or more. Now it's a cliché," Larry acknowledged.

"Did you ever think that God may be trying to get you in a complex situation where you can really make a difference in lives? Where you can love and not mix yourself up in self-pity and loneliness?" Evan paused for Larry's reaction.

"I suppose that it has crossed my mind, but there's Christine—and Pam would never want an old man. Why I'm old enough to be her children's grandfather."

"Did you ask her?" Evan asked.

"You know I haven't," Larry admitted.

"Please, my friend, when you say your prayers ask the Good Lord to grant you the wisdom to know yourself," Evan declared. "And everything will fall into place, I guarantee it." Evan fondly put his arms around Larry's shoulders.

While Larry was packing Evan's take-home cake he stopped and looked up, "Evan," he said seriously, "what about Christine?"

Evan said, "Ah yes, Christine." He looked heavenward and stretched out his arms. "I can see her now. She's tapping another angel on the shoulder and pointing, 'That's my Larry, I'm so proud of him.'"

Larry walked to the door and held it for Evan, "Thanks," he said.

"Have I helped?" Evan asked as he gazed into Larry's face.

Larry nodded his head and answered, "Yes."

＊　　　＊　　　＊　　　＊

Larry hadn't agreed totally with Evan, but clearly his conscience was still burdened. He arose early the next morning and drove to Gaffney.

Searching Larry's eyes, Pam said, "You look as though you didn't sleep a wink last night."

"I didn't," Larry said.

"Why don't you have some breakfast?" Pam suggested.

"Yes, my usual—light on the grease," he said.

"Add an extra egg to the plain omelette," Pam told the cook.

While he was eating she told him that the doctor had said that the baby was doing fine and now seemed very active.

"Pam …" Larry said, "could you or Loren call me the instant you go to the hospital? I want to be there with you," he said seriously and added, "promise?"

Pam nodded.

"And tell the boys that I'm coming as soon as possible to take them to McDonald's."

CHAPTER 21

▼

Larry had been on a business call to Columbia, South Carolina. On his way home he stopped by Sam Simmons' office.

"Hello, Mister Foster, how are you?" Susan asked.

"Good afternoon, Susan, I'm fine. I see you're as pretty as ever," Larry replied, smiling. "Is Sam in?"

"Yes, sir. One moment, please," Susan said as she pushed the intercom button. "Mister Foster, from Flat Rock, is here to see you."

"Send him on in," Larry heard Sam say.

"Well, well, how's our traveling adventurer?" Sam said jovially as he shook Larry's hand.

"I've never thought of my job exactly that way, but I'm fine, thanks."

"Oh, my friend, I would think every day would be an adventure for you. Different places, different girls, eh?" he elbowed Larry's ribs. "Why, even our staid and true Susan has a certain something in her voice when she announces you." Sam lifted his eyebrows as if to give creditability to his words.

Larry smiled and nodded his head, "Sam, we're into the eyes of the beholder again. It's a lonely and sometimes hectic life driving, in all kinds of weather, coming in late at night to cold motel rooms in strange places, trying to make appointments for fear of losing commissions—the list goes on and on. But I didn't come to burn up your time," Larry began taking a blank check from his wallet.

"I understand," Sam said. "We're always looking in the other man's pasture. By the way, how's your surrogate? I think her name is Pamela. How's she doing?"

"Pam's a wonder. You'd never suspect that she's carrying a baby, not as far along as she is," Larry said proudly.

"Now let's see, she's in her last trimester?" Sam asked, trying to think back to when she was inseminated.

"Smack in the middle of it. It's gonna be a small baby, but the doctor says the baby's healthy."

"That's good. So it won't be long until you're a father?"

Larry was tired from the long drive from Columbia and wanted to get on with the business, "Not long," he said. "I thought that I would stop by since I was passing through Spartanburg to give you a check."

Sam looked puzzled, "For?"

"The contract. I want to pay it off," Larry explained.

Sam didn't understand, "But, my friend, it's too early. We have your deposit."

"No, I want to pay off the contract. Your job is done. I want to clear off the table," Larry insisted.

"Our commission, too?" Sam asked.

"Everything, Sam. I like you and your office, but I don't like things hanging over my head—especially debts."

"But you don't have the baby yet. She might change her mind, women do …" Sam warned.

"That would be her conscience. I'm only responsible for me," Larry said with a wry half-smile.

"There could be something wrong with the baby," Sam was thinking of all the things that could go wrong.

"I don't think so," Larry answered. "If so, I'll deal with it," he vowed.

"But she might decide to go to court, trying to block your getting the child." Sam's eyes were wide, "I'm your attorney in this matter."

"That you are, Sam. If I need a good South Carolina lawyer, you're my man," Larry held his ground. "But right now I want to pay my bill." Larry repeated.

"The commission, too?" Sam asked.

"Yes, the total bill on our completed contract."

Slowly Sam pushed the intercom button, "Susan, would you please make out a final contract statement for Mister Foster?" There was a pause as Sam listened, "Yes, Susan, include the thirty percent commission."

Then Sam turned to Larry, "What about the final payment to the surrogate?"

Larry scratched his head, "That, too," he answered.

"Susan, include that, too," Sam said.

"While we're waiting for Susan to do her thing, let's visit Betsy at the cafe. I need an afternoon pick-me-up," Sam smiled.

After coffee and Sam's pick-me-up Danish they returned to Sam's office.

Handing the blank check to Susan, Larry said, "You fill it out and I'll sign it."

*   *   *   *

As Larry was driving up the Saluda grade he was thinking of Sam's mentioning the final payoff to the surrogate. He kept going back in his mind, trying to remember, but for the life of him he couldn't recall his discussing the payoff with Pam.

When he got home he called Sam. "Hello, Sam, this is Larry Foster. In the agreement with Pamela Adcock, what did we put down as the final payoff figure?" Larry asked.

"Don't you remember—fifty thousand. It was your idea and she agreed."

"Thank you, Sam." Larry started to hang up.

"Larry, I was thinking ... you mentioned that the baby Pam is carrying is small."

"Yes, it is," Larry answered.

"And it's her fifth birth, right?" Sam asked.

"Yes, her fifth. Why?" Larry asked.

"My friend, if it was her first I wouldn't say this, but fifth? You'd better be prepared for an early birth. I'll give you odds that the baby comes early," Sam chuckled over the phone.

"I don't think so. Everything so far is right on schedule," Larry answered.

"You have the nursery ready?" Sam warned.

"Everything's taken care of, Sam. Not to worry," Larry said. "You're happy with your check?" he added as an afterthought.

"Delighted, my friend. You're a good man to do business with," Sam responded.

*   *   *   *

Larry's last thought that night before drifting off to sleep was Sam's warning about the baby coming early. *What in the world is going on?* He thought. *Is that fire alarm ringing? Is the house on fire?* His eyes refused to open. He shook his head, trying to focus on the illumed clock dial. Did he set the alarm on the clock? All these things were running through his mind as he struggled to consciousness.

It was still dark and it was the phone ringing he finally figured out. "Hello," he said groggily.

"Hello ... Mister Foster?" a woman's voice asked with anxiety.

"Yes, yes," he answered.

"This is Loren, Pam's sister."

"Has something happened to Pam?" Instantly he was alert and rushed his words, thinking that she might have had a miscarriage.

"She just left in an ambulance for the hospital," Loren answered.

"Is she all right?" Larry's voice was nervous.

"I don't know, Mister Foster. She began having pains last night. I told her she had better go to the hospital, but she wanted to wait until morning," Loren said.

"What happened to change her mind?" Larry asked.

"Her water broke. She called me, I called the ambulance. I'm at her house, minding the boys," Loren said.

"I'll get dressed and hurry on down," Larry said.

"I don't think you'll make it, Mister Foster," Loren warned.

"What are you talking about?" Larry asked.

"That baby is in a hurry, too. I think that it will beat you to the hospital," Loren guessed.

Larry dressed, threw his overnight bag into the car trunk and raced down the mountain. Several times he forced himself to slow down. He was aware that patrolmen watched all through the night to catch speeders.

He had previously checked out the location of the Gaffney Hospital—just in case. After parking in the Emergency area he ran up the hospital stairs and then to the front desk. "Pamela Adcock's room, please," he blurted out.

The desk attendant checked her rotary index, "Room 205," she said.

"Thanks," Larry shouted over his shoulder as he ran under the stairway sign. Room 205 was the third door on the left. Cautiously he eased the door open.

There was Pam, cradling a tiny baby in her arms. "Larry," she exclaimed, "come look at your daughter," she said.

He inched toward the bed as Pam tenderly opened the baby blanket so that he could see. "Isn't she beautiful?" She tried to smile bravely, but tears overtook her as she began sobbing.

"Why are you crying?" Larry asked for he never could abide a woman's tears. His eyes began to well.

"Because she's what I've always wanted and you're going to take her away from me. Oh, Larry, I can't give her up. I'll wash floors, do anything to pay you back. Please don't make me give her up," Pam pleaded.

He bent over the bed and looked into her eyes. "Pam, listen, don't cry. I could never take a baby from its mother, certainly not my own daughter. I just could never do that." He looked at her, hoping his words would soak in and remembering Evan Charles' remark about his knowing himself.

"But what are we going to do?" she sobbed. "She needs her father."

Larry took a tissue from the box beside the bed and dabbed at Pam's tears. "My daughter needs her mother," he said with feeling.

"Oh, I can't stop crying. You take her, I don't want her to see me crying," Pam said through her tears.

"The baby's eyes are closed. I'm the one that's suffering through the tears," Larry said as he gently put his hand behind the baby's head and nestled it against his chest. "She feels like a five pound bag of sugar," he said, remembering Evan Charles' remarks about a little levity lightening up a tearful situation.

"That's what she weighs—five pounds and four ounces," Pam sniffed and again burst into tears.

"Why are you crying now? I promised not to take her," he said.

"But you … you look so daddy-like holding her," Pam got the words out between sobs. She reached out her hand and touched his arm, "I have an idea that would solve everything," she managed to say through her tears.

"What?" he asked, searching her wet blue eyes.

"We … we could … get married," she hesitated before saying the words.

Larry stepped back, still gently patting the baby, "You don't want to marry me," he exclaimed, shaking his head.

"Yes, I do. It's the perfect solution," she said, getting another tissue and wiping her eyes.

"I'm old enough to be your father," he protested.

"No, you're not," she shook her head.

"I'm over fifty," he exclaimed.

Pam kept shaking her head. "No, you're not. That's calendar years. In living years, you're forty—tops. 'round my boys, much younger than that," she managed to add.

Larry didn't know what to say.

"And to me you're the exact age as Prince Charming," she said as she pulled the man holding her baby close to her face. "I love you, Larry Foster … my boys love you and … our new daughter loves you." She softly kissed his lips.

Larry looked into her eyes, then abruptly straightened. "Stop it," he said, "or else I'll be crying. Our daughter wouldn't like that," as he held the baby's warm head against his cheek. He took Pam's hand, saying, "I've learned two things about myself."

"What, darling?" Pam asked.

"For one, I could never take a baby from its mother."
"And the second thing?" Pam asked, sincerely wanting to know.
"That I'm a push-over for McDonald's," Larry smiled.

✳   ✳   ✳   ✳

As the searching ends—the adventure begins.

"Happy Ending"

978-0-595-47179-9
0-595-47179-X

www.ingramcontent.com/pod-product-compliance
Lightning Source LLC
Chambersburg PA
CBHW051844170626
46807CB00003B/1336